**The Magical Adventures of**
**The Worst Witch**

*The Worst Witch*

*The Worst Witch Strikes Again*

*A Bad Spell for the Worst Witch*

*The Worst Witch at Sea*

*The Worst Witch Saves the Day*

*The Worst Witch to the Rescue*

*The Worst Witch and the Wishing Star*

# THREE CHEERS FOR
# THE WORST WITCH

## JILL MURPHY

CANDLEWICK PRESS

*The Worst Witch* copyright © 1974 by Jill Murphy
*The Worst Witch Strikes Again* copyright © 1980 by Jill Murphy
*A Bad Spell for the Worst Witch* copyright © 1982 by Jill Murphy

First edition in this format 2017

*The Worst Witch*
Library of Congress Catalog Card Number 99054542
ISBN 978-0-7636-1254-2 (paperback)
ISBN 978-0-7636-7260-7 (revised paperback)

*The Worst Witch Strikes Again*
Library of Congress Catalog Card Number 99056240
ISBN 978-0-7636-1255-9 (paperback)
ISBN 978-0-7636-7257-7 (revised paperback)

*A Bad Spell for the Worst Witch*
Library of Congress Catalog Card Number 99055051
ISBN 978-0-7636-1256-6 (paperback)
ISBN 978-0-7636-7252-2 (revised paperback)

ISBN 978-0-7636-9897-3 (paperback bindup)

17 18 19 20 21 22 BVG 10 9 8 7 6 5 4 3 2 1

Printed in Berryville, VA, U.S.A.

This book was typeset in Baskerville.
The illustrations were done in ink.

Candlewick Press
99 Dover Street
Somerville, Massachusetts 02144

visit us at www.candlewick.com

# CONTENTS

For Reeeney

# CHAPTER ONE

ISS CACKLE'S Academy for Witches stood at the top of a high mountain surrounded by a pine forest. It looked more like a prison than a school, with its gloomy grey walls and turrets. Sometimes you could see the pupils on their broomsticks flitting like bats above the playground wall, but usually the place was half hidden in mist, so that if you had glanced up at the mountain you would probably not have noticed the building was there at all.

Everything about the school was dark and shadowy. There were long, narrow corridors and winding staircases — and of course there were the girls themselves, dressed in black gymslips, black stockings, black hobnailed boots, grey shirts and black-and-grey ties. Even their summer dresses were black-and-grey checked. The only touches of colour were the sashes round their gymslips — a different colour for each house — and the school badge, which was a black cat sitting on a yellow moon. For special occasions, such as prize-giving or Hallowe'en, there was another uniform consisting of a long robe worn with a tall, pointed hat, but as these were black too, it didn't really make much of a change.

There were so many rules that you couldn't do *any*thing without being told off, and there seemed to be tests and exams every week.

Mildred Hubble was in her first year at the school. She was one of those people who always seem to be in trouble. She didn't exactly mean to break rules and annoy the teachers, but things just seemed to *happen* whenever she was around. You could rely on Mildred to have her hat on back-to-front or her bootlaces trailing along the floor. She couldn't walk from one end of a corridor to the other without someone yelling at her, and nearly every night she was writing lines or being kept in (not that there was anywhere to go if you were allowed out). Anyway, she had lots of friends, even if they did keep their distance in the potion laboratory, and her best friend, Maud, stayed loyally by her through everything, however hair-raising. They made a funny pair, for Mildred was tall and thin with long plaits, which she often chewed absentmindedly (another thing she was told off about), while Maud was short and tubby, had round glasses, and wore her hair in bunches.

On her first day at the academy, each pupil was given a broomstick and taught to ride it, which takes quite a long time and isn't nearly as easy as it looks. Halfway through the first term they were each presented with a black kitten, which they trained to ride the broomsticks. The cats weren't for any practical purpose except to keep tradition going; some schools present owls instead, but it's just a matter of taste. Miss Cackle was a very traditional headmistress who did not believe in any newfangled nonsense and trained her young witches to keep up all the customs that had been taught in her young day. At the end of the first year, each pupil received a copy of *The Popular Book of Spells*, a three-inch thick volume bound in black leather. This was not really to be used, as they already had paperback editions for the

classroom, but like the cats it was another
piece of tradition. Apart from yearly
prize-giving, there were no more presen-
tations until the fifth and final year, when
most pupils were awarded the Witches'
Higher Certificate. It did not seem likely
that Mildred would ever get that far. After
only two days at the school she crashed
her broomstick into the yard wall, break-
ing the broomstick in half and bending
her hat. She mended the stick with glue
and sticky tape, and fortunately it still flew,
though there was an ugly bundle where
the ends joined and sometimes it was rather
difficult to control.

This story really begins halfway through Mildred's first term, on the night before the presentation of the kittens. . . .

It was almost midnight and the school was in darkness except for one narrow window lit softly by the glow of a candle. This was Mildred's room, where she was sitting in bed, wearing a pair of black-and-grey striped pyjamas and dropping off to sleep every few minutes. Maud was curled up on the end of the bed, enveloped in a grey flannel nightdress and a black woollen shawl. Each pupil had the same type of room: very simple, with a wardrobe, iron bedstead, table, and chair, and a slit window like the ones used by archers in castles of long ago. There was a picture rail along the bare walls, from which hung a sampler embroidered with a quotation from *The Book of Spells* and also, during the day, several bats. Mildred had three bats in her room, little furry

ones which were very friendly. She was fond of animals and was looking forward to the next day when she would have a kitten of her own. Everyone was very excited about the presentation, and they had all spent the evening ironing their best robes and pushing the dents out of their best hats. Maud was too excited to sleep, so had sneaked into Mildred's room to talk about it with her friend.

"What are you going to call yours, Maud?" asked Mildred, sleepily.

"Midnight," said Maud. "I think it sounds dramatic."

"I'm worried about the whole thing," Mildred confessed, chewing the end of her plait. "I'm sure I'll do something dreadful like treading on its tail, or else it'll take one look at me and leap out of the window. *Some*thing's bound to go wrong."

"Don't be silly," said Maud. "You know you have a way with animals. And as for treading on its tail, it won't even be on the floor. Miss Cackle hands it to you, and that's all there is to it. So there's nothing to worry about, is there?"

Before Mildred had time to reply, the door crashed open to reveal their form mistress, Miss Hardbroom, standing in the doorway wrapped in a black dressing

gown, with a lantern in her hand. She was
a tall, terrifying lady with a sharp, bony
face and black hair scragged back into

such a tight knot that her forehead looked quite stretched.

"Rather late to be up, isn't it, girls?" she inquired nastily.

The girls, who had leapt into each other's arms when the door burst open, drew apart and fixed their eyes on the floor.

"Of course, if we don't want to be included in the presentation tomorrow we are certainly going about it the right way," Miss Hardbroom continued icily.

"Yes, Miss Hardbroom," chorused the girls miserably.

Miss Hardbroom glared meaningfully at Mildred's candle and swept out into the corridor with Maud in front of her.

Mildred hastily blew out the candle and dived under the bedclothes, but she could not get to sleep. Outside the window she could hear the owls hooting, and somewhere in the school a door had been left open and was creaking backwards and forwards in the wind. To tell you the truth, Mildred was afraid of the dark, but don't tell anyone. I mean, whoever heard of a *witch* who was scared of the dark?

# CHAPTER TWO

HE PRESENTATION took place in the Great Hall, a huge stone room with rows of wooden benches, a raised platform at one end, and shields and portraits all round the walls. The whole school had assembled, and Miss Cackle and Miss Hardbroom stood behind a table on the platform. On the table was a large wicker basket from which came mews and squeaks.

First of all everyone sang the school song, which went like this:

*Onward, ever striving onward,*
*Proudly on our brooms we fly*
*Straight and true above the treetops,*
*Shadows on the moonlit sky.*

*Ne'er a day will pass before us*
*When we have not tried our best,*
*Kept our cauldrons bubbling nicely,*
*Cast our spells and charms with zest.*

*Full of joy we mix our potions,*
*Working by each other's side.*
*When our days at school are over*
*Let us think of them with pride.*

It was the usual type of school song, full of pride, joy, and striving. Mildred had never yet mixed a potion with joy, nor flown her broomstick with pride—she was usually too busy trying to keep upright!

Anyway, when they had finished droning the last verse, Miss Cackle rang the little silver bell on her table and the girls marched up in single file to receive their kittens. Mildred was the last of all, and when she reached the table Miss Cackle pulled out of the basket not a sleek black kitten like all the others but a little tabby with white paws and the sort of fur that looked as if it had been out all night in a gale.

"We ran out of black ones," explained Miss Cackle with a pleasant grin.

Miss Hardbroom smiled too, but nastily.

After the ceremony everyone rushed to see Mildred's kitten.

"I think H.B. had a hand in this somewhere," said Maud darkly. ("H.B." was their nickname for Miss Hardbroom.)

"I must admit, it does look a bit dim,

doesn't it?" said Mildred, scratching the tabby kitten's head. "But I don't really mind. I'll just have to think of another name—I was going to call it Sooty. Let's take them down to the playground and see what they make of broomstick riding."

Almost all the first-year witches were in the yard trying to persuade their puzzled kittens to sit on their broomsticks. Several were already clinging on by their claws, and one kitten, belonging to a rather smug young witch named Ethel, was sitting bolt upright cleaning its paws, as if it had been broomstick riding all its life!

Riding a broomstick was no easy matter, as I have mentioned before. First, you ordered the stick to hover, and it hovered lengthways above the ground. Then you sat on it, gave it a sharp tap, and away you flew. Once in the air you could make the stick do almost anything by saying, "Right! Left! Stop! Down a bit!" and so on. The difficult part was balancing, for if you leaned a little too far to one side you could easily overbalance, in which case you would either fall off or find yourself hanging upside down and then you would just have to hold on with your skirt over your head until a friend came to your rescue.

It had taken Mildred several weeks of falling off and crashing before she could ride the broomstick reasonably well, and it looked as though her kitten was going to have the same trouble. When she put it on the end of the stick, it just fell off without even trying to hold on. After many attempts, Mildred picked up her kitten and gave it a shake.

"Listen!" she said severely. "I think I shall have to call you Stupid. You don't even *try* to hold on. Everyone else is all right — look at all your friends."

The kitten gazed at her sadly and licked her nose with its rough tongue.

"Oh, come on," said Mildred, softening

her voice. "I'm not really angry with you. Let's try again."

And she put the kitten back on the broomstick, from which it fell with a thud.

Maud was having better luck. Her kitten was hanging on grimly upside down.

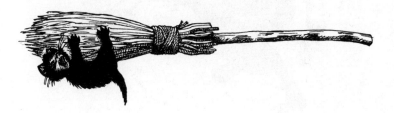

"Oh, well," laughed Maud. "It's a start."

"Mine's useless," said Mildred, sitting on the broomstick for a rest.

"Never mind," Maud said. "Think how hard it must be for them to hang on by their claws."

An idea flashed into Mildred's head, and she dived into the school, leaving her kitten chasing a leaf along the ground and the broomstick still patiently hovering.

She came out carrying her satchel, which she hooked over the end of the broom and then bundled the kitten into it. The kitten's astounded face peeped out of the bag as Mildred flew delightedly round the yard.

"Look, Maud!" she called from ten feet up in the air.

"That's cheating!" said Maud, looking at the satchel.

Mildred flew back and landed on the ground, laughing.

"I don't think H.B. will approve," said Maud doubtfully.

"Quite right, Maud," an icy voice behind them said. "Mildred, my dear, possibly it would be even easier with handlebars and a saddle."

Mildred blushed.

"I'm sorry, Miss Hardbroom," she muttered. "It doesn't balance very well—my kitten, so . . . I thought . . . perhaps . . ." Her voice trailed away under Miss Hardbroom's stony glare, and Mildred unhooked her satchel and turned the bewildered kitten onto the ground.

"Girls!" Miss Hardbroom clapped her hands. "I would remind you that there is a potion test tomorrow morning. That is all."

So saying, she disappeared—literally.

"I wish she wouldn't do that," whispered Maud, looking at the place where their form mistress had been standing. "You're never quite sure whether she's gone or not."

"Right again, Maud," came Miss Hardbroom's voice from nowhere.

Maud gulped and hurried back to her kitten.

# CHAPTER THREE

 O YOU remember I told you about a certain young witch named Ethel who had succeeded in teaching her kitten from the very first try? Ethel was one of those lucky people for whom everything goes right. She was always top of the class, her spells always worked, and Miss Hardbroom never made any icy remarks to her. Because of this, Ethel was often rather bossy with the other girls.

On this occasion she had overheard the whole of Mildred's encounter with Miss Hardbroom and couldn't resist being nasty about it.

"I think Miss Cackle gave you that cat on purpose," Ethel sneered. "You're both as bad as each other."

"Oh, be quiet," said Mildred, trying to keep her temper. "Anyway, it's not a bad cat. It'll learn in time."

"Like you did?" Ethel went on. "Wasn't it last week that you crashed into the dust-bins?"

"*Look*, Ethel," Mildred said, "you'd better be quiet, because if you don't, I shall . . ."

"Well?"

"I shall have to turn you into a frog— and I don't want to do that."

Ethel gave a shriek of laughter.

"That's really funny!" she crowed. "You don't even know the beginners' spells, let alone ones like that."

Mildred blushed and looked very miserable.

"Go on, then!" cried Ethel. "Go *on*,

then, if you're so clever. *Turn* me into a frog! I'm waiting."

It just so happened that Mildred did have an idea of that spell (she had been reading about it in the library). By now, everyone had crowded round, waiting to see what would happen, and Ethel was still jeering. It was unbearable.

Mildred muttered the spell under her

breath and Ethel vanished. In her place stood a small pink and grey pig.

Cries and shouts rent the air:

"Oh, no!"

"That's torn it!"

"You've done it now, Mildred!"

Mildred was horrified. "Oh, Ethel," she said. "I'm sorry, but you did ask for it."

The pig looked furious.

"You *beast*, Mildred Hubble!" it grunted. "Change me back!"

At that moment Miss Hardbroom suddenly appeared in the middle of the yard.

"Where is Ethel Hallow?" she asked. "Miss Bat would like to see her about extra chanting lessons."

Her sharp gaze fell on the small pig which was grunting softly at her feet.

"What is this animal doing in the yard?" she asked, coldly.

Everyone looked at Mildred.

"I . . . let it in, Miss Hardbroom," Mildred said hesitantly.

"Well, you can just let it out again, please," said Miss Hardbroom.

"Oh, I can't do that!" gasped the unhappy Mildred. "I mean, well . . . er . . . Couldn't I keep it as a pet?"

"I think you have quite enough trouble coping with yourself and that kitten without adding a pig to your worries," replied Miss Hardbroom, staring at the tabby kitten which was peering round Mildred's ankles. "Let it out at once! Now, where is Ethel?"

Mildred bent down.

"Ethel, dear," she whispered coaxingly in the pig's ear. "Will you go out when I tell you to? Please, Ethel, I'll let you in again straightaway afterwards."

Pleading with people like Ethel never works. It only makes them feel their power.

"I *won't* go!" bellowed the pig. "Miss Hardbroom, I *am* Ethel! Mildred Hubble turned me into a pig."

Nothing ever surprised Miss Hardbroom. Even this startling piece of news only caused her to raise one slanting eyebrow.

"Well, Mildred," she said, "I am glad to know that you have at least learned *one* thing since you came here. However, as you will have noticed in the Witches' Code, rule number seven, paragraph two, it is not customary to practise such tricks on your fellows. Please remove the spell at once."

"I'm afraid I don't know how to," Mildred confessed, in a very small voice.

Miss Hardbroom stared at her for a few moments.

"Then you had better go and look it up in the library," she said, wearily. "Take Ethel with you, and on your way drop in and tell Miss Bat why Ethel will be late."

Mildred picked up her kitten and hurried inside, followed by the pig. Fortunately, Miss Bat was not in her room, but it was most embarrassing going into the library. Ethel was grunting loudly on purpose and

everyone stared so much that Mildred could have crawled under the table.

"Hurry up," moaned the pig.

"Oh, stop going on!" said Mildred, as she flicked hastily through the huge spell book. "It's all your fault, anyway. You actually *asked* me to do it. I don't see why you're complaining."

"I said a frog, not a pig," said Ethel, pettily. "You couldn't even do *that* right."

Mildred ignored the grunting Ethel and kept looking in the book. It took her half an hour to find the right spell, and soon after that Ethel was her horrible self again. The people in the library were most surprised to see the pig suddenly change into a furious-looking Ethel.

"Now, don't be angry, Ethel," Mildred said softly. "Remember: 'Silence in the library at all times.' "

And she rushed into the corridor. "Wasn't that awful, Cat?" she said to the kitten, which was curled up inside her cardigan. "I think I'd better put you in my room and then go and revise for the potion test. Don't tease the bats, will you?"

# CHAPTER FOUR

 IT WAS the morning of the potion test, and the girls were filing into the potion lab, each hoping she had learned the right spell, except for Ethel who knew everything and never worried about such matters.

"Come along, girls! Two to a cauldron!" barked Miss Hardbroom. "Today we shall make a laughter potion. No textbooks to be used—put that book away this *instant*, Mildred! Work quietly, and when you have finished you may take a small sip of the mixture to make sure it is correctly made. You may begin."

Maud and Mildred were sharing a cauldron, of course, but unfortunately neither of them had learned that particular spell.

"I think I can remember it vaguely," whispered Maud. "Bits of it, anyway." She began to sort through the ingredients, which had been laid out on each workbench.

When everything was stirred together in the cauldron, the bubbling liquid was bright pink. Mildred stared at it doubtfully.

"I'm sure it should be green," she said. "In fact I'm sure we should have put in a handful of pondweed-gathered-at-midnight."

"Are you *sure?*" asked Maud.

"Yes . . ." replied Mildred, not very definitely.

"*Absolutely* sure?" Maud asked again. "You know what happened last time."

"I'm *quite* sure," insisted Mildred.

"Anyway, there's a handful of pondweed laid out on each bench. I'm positive we're supposed to put it in."

"Oh, all right," said Maud. "Go on, then. It can't do any harm."

Mildred grabbed the pondweed and dropped it into the mixture. They took turns at stirring it for a few minutes until it began to turn dark green.

"What a horrid colour," said Maud.

"Are you ready, girls?" asked Miss Hardbroom, rapping on her desk. "You should have been ready minutes ago. A laughter potion should be made quickly for use in an emergency."

Ethel was still working on the bench in front of Mildred, who stood on tiptoe to sneak a look at the colour of Ethel's potion. To her horror, it was bright pink.

"Oh, no," Mildred thought, with a sinking feeling. "I wonder what potion we've made?"

Miss Hardbroom banged on the desk again.

"We shall now test the potion," she commanded. "Not too much, please. We don't want anyone hysterical."

Each pupil took a test tubeful of liquid

and drank a little. At once shrieks of laughter rang through the room, especially from Ethel's bench, where they had made the best potion of all and were laughing so much that tears rolled down their cheeks. The only two girls who weren't laughing were Mildred and Maud.

"Oh, dear," said Maud. "I feel most peculiar. Why aren't we laughing, Mil?"

"I hate to tell you," confessed Mildred. "I think —" But before she had time to say any more, the two girls had disappeared!

"Cauldron number two!" snapped Miss Hardbroom. "You seem to have made the wrong spell."

"It was my fault," said Mildred's voice from behind the cauldron.

"That I do not doubt," Miss Hardbroom said sourly. "You had both better sit down until you reappear, and then, Mildred, perhaps a trip to Miss Cackle's office would do you some good. You can explain why I sent you."

Everyone had left the room by the time the two young witches finally began to reappear. This was a very slow process, with first the head and then the rest of the body becoming gradually visible.

"I'm sorry," said Mildred's head and shoulders.

"That's all right," said Maud's head. "I just wish you'd *think* a bit more. We had the right potion to start with."

"Sorry," mumbled Mildred again, then she began to laugh. "Hey, Maud, you do look funny with just your head showing!" At once they both began to laugh, and soon they were best friends again.

"I suppose I'd better go and see Old Cackle now," said Mildred, when she had completely reappeared.

"I'll come with you to the door," offered Maud.

Miss Cackle was small and very fat, with short grey hair and green horn-rimmed glasses, which she usually wore pushed up on top of her head. She was the exact opposite of Miss Hardbroom, being absentminded in appearance and rather gentle by nature. The girls were not in the least bit afraid of her, whereas Miss Hardbroom could reduce any of them to a miserable heap with just one word. Miss Cackle used a different technique. By always being friendly and pleased to see a pupil in her office, she made them feel embarrassed if they had something unpleasant to tell her, as Mildred nearly always had.

Mildred knocked at Miss Cackle's door, hoping she would be out. She wasn't.

"Come in!" called the familiar voice from inside.

Mildred opened the door and went in. Miss Cackle, glasses on her nose for once, was busily writing in a huge register. She looked up and peered over her spectacles.

"Ah, Mildred," she said pleasantly. "Come and sit down while I finish filling in this register."

Mildred closed the door and sat by Miss Cackle's desk.

"I wish she wasn't so pleased to see me," she thought.

Miss Cackle slammed the register shut and pushed her glasses onto the top of her head.

"Now, Mildred, what can I do for you?"
Mildred twisted her fingers together.

"Well, actually, Miss Cackle," she began
slowly, "Miss Hardbroom sent me to see you
because I made the wrong potion again."

The smile faded from the headmistress's face and she sighed, as if with deep disappointment. Mildred felt about an inch high.

"*Really,* Mildred," Miss Cackle said in a tired voice, "I have run out of things to say to you. Week after week you come here, sent by every member of staff in the school, and my words just seem to go straight in one ear and out of the other. You will never get the Witches' Higher Certificate if this appalling conduct continues. You must be the worst witch in the entire school. Whenever there's any trouble you are nearly always to be found at the bottom of it, and it's just not good enough, my dear. Now, what have you to say for yourself *this* time?"

"I don't really know, Miss Cackle," Mildred said humbly. "Everything I do just seems to go wrong, that's all. I don't *mean* to do it."

"Well, that's no excuse, is it?" said Miss Cackle. "Everyone else manages to live without causing an uproar wherever they go. You must pull yourself together, Mildred. I don't want to hear *any* more bad reports about you, do you understand?"

"Yes, Miss Cackle," said Mildred, in as sorry a voice as she could manage.

"Run along, then," said the headmistress, "and remember what I have said to you."

Maud was waiting in the corridor, eager to know what had been said, when her friend came out of the office.

"She's nice, really," Mildred said. "Just told me all the usual things. She hates telling people off. I'll have to try to be better from now on. Come on, let's go and give the kittens another broomstick lesson."

# CHAPTER FIVE

**T**HE FOLLOWING morning, Miss Hardbroom strode into the classroom looking thoughtful. She was wearing a new grey-and-black striped dress, with a brooch at the shoulder.

"Good morning, girls," she greeted them, not as sharply as usual.

"Good morning, Miss Hardbroom," chorused the girls.

Their form mistress arranged the books on her desk and surveyed the class.

"I have something to tell you, girls," she began, "that gives me great pleasure on one hand, yet causes me some worry on the other." Here she shot a glance at Mildred. "As you know, the Hallowe'en celebrations take place in two weeks' time, and it is customary for a display to be presented by this school. This year, our class has been chosen to present the display."

There were gasps of delight from the girls.

"Of course," Miss Hardbroom went on, "it is a great honour, but also a responsibility, as Miss Cackle's Academy has a very high reputation, which we don't want to spoil, *do we?* Last year, Form Three produced a play which was highly praised, and I thought that this year we might present a broomstick formation team. You will need a lot of practice, as some of you are not too steady on your broomsticks yet, but I am quite certain that we could give an interesting and successful performance. Is there anyone who would prefer something different?"

She looked round piercingly at the girls, who all shrank into their seats and would not have dared to disagree, even if they had wanted to.

"Good," said Miss Hardbroom. "Then it is settled. We shall present a broomstick formation team. Let us go down to the yard and begin to practise at once. Fetch your broomsticks and be outside in two minutes." With which words she vanished.

The girls excitedly clattered from the room and rushed along the corridors to fetch their broomsticks, which were kept in their own rooms. The spiral staircase rang with the sound of hobnailed boots as the girls rushed down to the yard, where they found Miss Hardbroom waiting for them.

"First of all, you'd better take a practise

flight," she said. "Form an orderly crocodile and go round the school and back."

Off they all flew in an orderly, but rather wobbly, procession round the school.

"Quite good, girls," said Miss Hardbroom, as they lined up in front of her. "You were swaying about rather badly, Mildred, but apart from that, you all did quite well. Now, I have made out a list of the things you will be doing. First, a single line, with each pupil sinking and rising alternately. This should be comparatively easy. Secondly, a flying 'V' similar to wild geese in flight. Then, nose-diving the yard and swooping up just before you reach the ground. That will be the most difficult part of all." Mildred and Maud exchanged horrified glances. "And finally you will form a circle in the air, each broomstick touching the next. Any questions? No? Very well, then, we shall begin the first

item immediately. What *was* the first item,
Mildred?"

". . . er, nose-diving the yard, Miss
Hardbroom."

"Wrong. Ethel, do you remember?"

"We are to form a line, each pupil sinking and rising alternately," replied Ethel,
word-perfect as always.

"Correct," said Miss Hardbroom, with a
frosty glare at Mildred. "We shall practise
all this morning and every morning until
the celebrations, and perhaps this afternoon, if I can persuade Miss Bat to allow
you to miss your chanting lesson."

They worked very hard for the next two weeks. Every spare minute was spent practising and, by the time Hallowe'en arrived, the display was quite a joy to watch. Maud's hat was squashed like a concertina from the time when she had not pulled up from a nose dive during practice, but apart from that there had been hardly any trouble at all, even from Mildred, who was making a special effort to be good and thoughtful.

The day before Hallowe'en, Miss Hardbroom lined up her class in the yard to give them a few final words of advice.

"I am very pleased with you, girls," she said, almost pleasantly. "Now, you will be wearing your best robes tomorrow, so I hope they will be clean and pressed."

As she said this she caught sight of Mildred's broomstick.

"Mildred, why is there a bundle of sticky tape in the middle of your broomstick?"

"I'm afraid I broke it in half during the first week of term," admitted Mildred.

Ethel giggled.

"I see," said Miss Hardbroom. "Well, you certainly can't use that one in the display. Ethel, I seem to remember you have a spare one. Perhaps you could lend it to Mildred?"

"Oh, Miss Hardbroom!" cried Ethel. "It was given to me as a birthday present. I shouldn't want anything to happen to it."

Miss Hardbroom fixed Ethel with one of her nastiest looks.

"If that is how you feel, Ethel," she said in icy tones, "then —"

"Oh, I didn't mean I *won't* lend it, Miss Hardbroom," Ethel said, meekly. "I'll go and fetch it now." And she ran into the school.

Ethel had never forgotten the time Mildred had turned her into a pig, and as she made her way up the spiral staircase she suddenly thought of a marvellous way of taking her revenge. (Ethel really wasn't a nice person at all.)

"I'll fix you, Mildred Hubble," she cackled to herself, as she took the broomstick out of her cupboard. "Now, listen to me, Broom, this is very important . . ."

The class had dismissed when Ethel returned carrying the broomstick. Mildred was practising nose-diving the yard.

"Here's the broom, Mildred," called Ethel. "I'll leave it propped against the wall."

"Thanks very much," replied Mildred, delighted that Ethel was being so nice, for the two hadn't spoken since the pig episode. "It's very kind of you."

"Not at all," said Ethel, smiling wickedly to herself as she went back into the school.

# CHAPTER SIX

 HALLOWE'EN was celebrated each year in the ruins of an old castle quite near the school. The special fires were lit at sunset, and by dark all the witches and wizards had assembled.

As the sun set, the members of Miss Cackle's Academy were preparing to leave the school. Mildred smoothed her robes, said good-bye to her kitten, put on her hat, grabbed Ethel's broomstick, and ran down to the yard. She took a quick look out of her window before leaving the room and saw the fires being lit in the distance. It was very exciting.

The rest of the school had already assembled as Mildred rushed out of the door and took her place. Miss Hardbroom looked splendid in her full witch's robes and hat.

"Everyone is present now," Miss Hardbroom announced to Miss Cackle.

"Then we shall set off," said the head-mistress. "To the celebrations! Class Five first, Class Four second, and so on until Class One!"

They made a wonderful sight flying over the trees towards the castle, cloaks soaring in the wind, and the older girls with their cats perched on the ends of their broomsticks. Miss Hardbroom looked particularly impressive, sitting bolt-upright with her long black hair streaming behind her. The girls had never seen her hair loose before and were amazed how much of it she could possibly scrag into that tight knot every day. It came down to her waist.

"H.B. looks quite nice with her hair like that," whispered Maud to Mildred, who was riding next to her.

"Yes," agreed Mildred, "she doesn't seem half as frightening."

Miss Hardbroom turned round and shot a piercing look at the two girls.

"No talking!" she snapped.

A huge crowd was already there at the castle when they arrived. The pupils of the Academy lined up in neat rows while Miss Cackle and all the other teachers shook hands with the chief wizard. He was very old, with a long white beard and a purple gown embroidered with moons and stars.

"And what have you prepared for us this year?" he asked.

"We have prepared a broomstick formation team, Your Honour," Miss Cackle replied. "Shall we begin, Miss Hardbroom?"

Miss Hardbroom clapped her hands and the girls lined up, with Ethel at the front.

"You may begin," said Miss Hardbroom.

Ethel rose perfectly into the air, followed by the rest of the class. First, they made a line, sinking and rising, which received great applause. Then they nose dived the yard. (Miss Cackle closed her eyes during this part, but nothing went wrong.) Then the girls made a V in the air, which looked quite beautiful.

"Your girls get better every year," remarked a young witch to Miss Hardbroom, who smiled.

Last of all came the circle, which was quite the easiest part.

"All over soon," whispered Maud, arranging her broomstick in front of Mildred.

As soon as they had formed the circle,

Mildred knew that something was the matter with her broomstick. It started to rock about, and seemed to be trying to throw her off balance.

"Maud!" she cried to her friend. "There's something—" but before Mildred could say any more, the broomstick gave a violent kick like a bucking bronco and she fell off, grabbing at Maud as she fell.

There was chaos in the air. All the girls were screaming and clutching at each other, and soon there was a tangled mass of broomsticks and witches on the ground. The only girl who flew serenely back to earth was Ethel. A few of the younger witches laughed, but most of them looked grim.

"We are so sorry, Your Honour," apologized Miss Cackle, as Miss Hardbroom untangled the heap of girls and jerked them to their feet. "I'm sure there must be some simple explanation."

"Miss Cackle," said the chief magician

sternly, "your pupils are the witches of the future. I shudder to think what that future will be like."

He paused, and there was complete silence. Miss Hardbroom glared at Mildred.

"However," continued the chief magician, "we shall forget this incident for the rest of the evening. Let us now begin the chanting."

# CHAPTER SEVEN

A T DAWN the celebrations ended, and the pupils flew wearily back to school, some riding double as their own broomsticks were broken. No one was speaking to Mildred (even Maud was being very cool towards her friend), and Form One was in disgrace. When they arrived at the Academy, everyone was sent straight to bed. It was the custom, after the all-night Hallowe'en celebrations, to sleep until noon the next day.

"Mildred!" said Miss Cackle, in a sharp voice, as Form One made their way miserably up the stairs. "Miss Hardbroom and I will see you in my office first thing tomorrow afternoon."

"Yes, Miss Cackle," replied Mildred, almost in tears, and she ran up the steps.

As Mildred opened her bedroom door, Ethel, who was behind her, leaned across and whispered, "*That'll* teach you to go around changing people into pigs!" and she pulled a face and ran away down the corridor.

Mildred closed the door and fell onto her bed, almost flattening the kitten, which leapt out of the way just in time.

"Oh, Tabby," she said, burying her face in the kitten's warm fur, "I've had such a dreadful time, and it wasn't even my fault! I might have known Ethel wouldn't lend me her broomstick out of kindness.

Nobody will ever believe that it wasn't me just being clumsy as usual."

The kitten licked her ear sympathetically, and the bats returned through the narrow window and settled upside down on the picture rail.

Two hours later, Mildred was lying in bed, still wide awake. She was imagining what the interview with Miss Cackle and her terrible form mistress would be like. The kitten was curled up peacefully on her chest.

"It'll be *awful*," she thought, sadly looking towards the grey sky outside the window. "I wonder if they'll expel me? Or perhaps I could tell them that it was Ethel — no, I would never do that. Suppose they decide to turn me into a frog? No, I'm sure they wouldn't do anything like that; Miss Hardbroom said that was against the Witches' Code. Oh, what *will* they do to me? Even Maud thinks it's my fault, and I've never seen H.B. look more furious."

She lay thinking about it until she was really frightened, and suddenly she leapt out of bed.

"Come on, Tabby!" she said, pulling a bag out of the wardrobe. "We're running away."

She stuffed a few clothes and books into the bag and put on her best robe so that no one would recognize the usual school uniform. Then she picked up her broomstick, put the kitten into the bag, and crept out along the silent corridor to the spiral staircase.

"I shall miss the bats," she thought.

It was a cold, dull morning, and Mildred pulled her cape about her shoulders as she crossed the yard, glancing round in case anyone was watching. The school seemed very strange with no one about. Mildred had to fly over the gates, which were locked as usual, but it was difficult to balance with the bag slung on the back of her broomstick, so she got off on the other side of the gates and started through the pine trees on foot.

"I don't know where we're going, Tabby," she said, as they picked their way down the mountainside.

# CHAPTER EIGHT

IT WAS very gloomy in the forest, and Mildred felt slightly uneasy, surrounded by dark trees which grew so thickly together that no light fell between them. When she was almost at the bottom of the mountain, she sat down to rest, leaning her back against a tree, and the kitten climbed out of the bag to stretch itself on the grass.

It was very quiet except for a few birds singing, and a rather strange noise, a sort of low humming, almost like a lot of people talking at once. In fact, the more

Mildred listened, the more it did sound like voices. She looked in the direction of the noise and thought she saw something moving along the trees.

"Let's go and have a look, Tabby," she whispered.

They left the bag and broomstick leaning against the tree, and crept through the tangled undergrowth. The noise grew louder.

"Why, it *is* people talking," said Mildred. "Look, Tabby, over there, through the branches."

Sitting in a clearing in the gloom were about twenty witches, all crowded together, muttering and talking in low voices. Mildred crept nearer and listened. She didn't recognize any of them. A tall, grey-haired witch got to her feet.

"Listen, everyone," said the grey-haired witch. "Will you all be quiet for a few moments? Thank you. Now, what I should like to know is, are we quite sure that they will all be sleeping, or at least in their rooms?"

She sat down, and another witch got up to reply. She was a small, plump witch with green horn-rimmed glasses. For a horrible moment Mildred thought it was Miss Cackle, but her voice was different when she spoke.

"Of course we are sure," this witch replied. "The morning after Hallowe'en celebrations the entire school sleeps until midday. It is a rule, and the school is very strict about rules, so no one will be up until five minutes to twelve at the very earliest. If we fly over the wall into the back part of the yard, we will be as far away from the bedrooms as we can be, and no one will possibly hear us. Added to this, we shall all be invisible, so we shall be extremely well protected. Then all that remains to be done is to split up, sneak into each room, and turn them all into frogs. They

won't be able to see us even if they *are* awake. Remember to take one of these boxes with you for the frogs." She pointed to a neat pile of small cardboard boxes. "We can't have even one of them escaping.

Once this is done, the entire school and everyone in it will be under our control.

"Is the invisibility potion ready yet?" she continued, turning to a young witch who was stirring a cauldron over a fire. It was the same potion that the two Ms had made during the laughter potion test.

"Another few minutes," replied the young witch, dropping a handful of bats' whiskers into the mixture. "It needs to simmer for a bit."

Mildred was horrified. She sneaked back to where she had left her bag, and then into the shadows so that she couldn't be seen.

"What on earth can we do, Tab?" she whispered to the kitten, imagining Maud hopping about, turned into a frog. "We can't let them take over the school."

She rummaged through the bag and took out the two books she had brought with her. One was the Witches' Code and the other was her spell book. Mildred flicked through the spell book and stopped at the page about turning people into animals. There was only one example given, and that was snails.

"Dare I?" thought Mildred. "Dare I turn the whole lot of them into snails?" The kitten looked at her, encouragingly.

"I know it's against the Witches' Code, Tabby," she said, "but *they* don't seem to follow any rules. They were planning to change us into frogs while we were *asleep*, so I don't see why we shouldn't do the same to them in self-defence."

She sneaked back to the clearing, clutching her spell book.

"Here goes!" she thought desperately.

The invisibility potion was being poured out into cups, so Mildred had to work quickly. She waved her arms in a circle towards the crowd of witches (this part of spell making can be very awkward when

you don't want to draw attention to yourself) and muttered the spell under her
breath. For a second, nothing happened,
and the witches milling round the cauldron
continued to chatter and bustle about.
Mildred closed her eyes in despair, but
when she opened them again everyone had
vanished and on the ground was a group
of snails of all different shapes and sizes.

"Tabby!" shrieked Mildred. "I've done
it! Look!"

Tabby came bounding out of the undergrowth and stared at the snails, who were

all moving away as fast as they could, which wasn't very fast. Mildred took one of the cardboard boxes and put the snails into it, gently picking them up one by one.

"I suppose we'll have to take them back to school and tell Miss Cackle, Tab," she said, suddenly remembering her interview to come at noon. "Still, we'll have to go back. We can't just leave this lot here, can we?"

So they set off up the mountainside, Mildred carrying the box in her arms, while the broomstick flew alongside with the bag hanging from it and Tabby riding inside the bag.

# CHAPTER NINE

**T**HE SCHOOL was still completely deserted when Mildred arrived once more at the heavy iron gates. She hurried up the spiral staircase to her room and unpacked her bag so that no one would know she had tried to run away. Just as she was making her way to the door with the box in her arms, the door opened and Miss Hardbroom appeared.

"Would you kindly tell me what you are doing, Mildred?" she asked frostily. "I have just watched you creeping up the corridor, complete with broomstick, cat, a bag and this cardboard box. Is it too much to ask for an explanation?"

"Oh, no, Miss Hardbroom," replied Mildred, holding up the box for her form mistress to see the contents. "You see, I found a crowd of witches on the mountain-side, and they were planning to take over the school and change you all into frogs, and they were making an invisibility potion so you wouldn't be able to see them, so I turned them all into snails and brought . . ."

Her words trailed into silence as she saw the expression on Miss Hardbroom's face. Obviously, her form mistress didn't believe a word.

"I suppose these are the witches?" she asked bitterly, pointing to the snails which were all huddled up in one corner of the box.

"Yes, they are!" Mildred insisted des-perately. "I know it sounds a peculiar story, Miss Hardbroom, but you must believe me. Their broomsticks and cauldrons and things are still in the clearing where I found them. Really."

"Well, you had better show the creatures to Miss Cackle," said Miss Hardbroom, nastily. "Go and wait in Miss Cackle's office while I fetch her — and I hope this isn't any sort of joke, Mildred. I seem to remember that you are already in a considerable amount of trouble."

Mildred was perched nervously on the edge of a chair in the headmistress's office when Miss Hardbroom returned with Miss Cackle, who was wearing a grey dressing gown, and looked half asleep.

"*These* are they," stated Miss Hardbroom, pointing to the box on the desk.

Miss Cackle sat down heavily in her chair and looked first into the box and then at Mildred.

"Mildred," she said in dramatic tones, "I am still suffering from my public

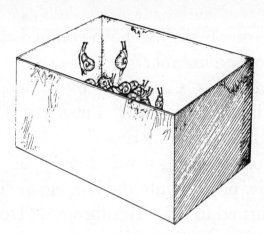

humiliation last night. Because of you the reputation of this school now lies in the mud, and yet you expect me to believe an incredible story like this?"

"But it's *true!*" cried Mildred. "I can even describe some of them. One was tall and thin with thick grey hair, and there was another who looked just like you, Miss Cackle, if you'll excuse me being personal. She had green horn-rimmed glasses —"

"Wait a moment!" said Miss Cackle, pushing her own glasses onto her nose.

"Did you say she had horn-rimmed glasses and looked like me?"

"Yes, Miss Cackle," replied Mildred, blushing. "Green ones. I'm sorry if you thought I was being rude."

"No, no, child, it isn't that," said Miss Cackle, peering into the box again. Then she turned to Miss Hardbroom. "Do you know, I think the girl may be right after all. The person whom she described sounds exactly like my wicked sister Agatha who has always been extremely jealous of my position at this Academy!"

Miss Cackle stared over her glasses at the snails.

"Well, well, Agatha," she chuckled. "So we meet again. I wonder which of these beauties you are? What shall we do with them, Miss Hardbroom?"

"I suggest we change them back to their natural form again."

"But we can't!" cried Miss Cackle in dismay. "There are *twenty* of them."

Miss Hardbroom looked faintly amused.

"May I point out," she said, "paragraph five of rule number seven in the Witches' Code, which states that anyone having been changed into any type of animal by another witch, for purposes of self-defence, cannot, on being changed back again, practise any form of magic against their captor. In other words, they must admit defeat."

Miss Cackle looked embarrassed.

"Oh, yes!" she said brightly. "I remember now. It slipped my mind for the moment. Did you hear that, Agatha? Do you think they can hear us, Miss Hardbroom?"

"Most certainly," replied Miss Hardbroom. "Perhaps you could line them up on your desk, and ask your sister to step forward?"

"What a splendid idea," said Miss Cackle, who was beginning to enjoy herself. "Help me, Mildred, my dear."

They lined the snails up on the desk and Miss Cackle asked Agatha to step forward. One snail shuffled rather reluctantly out of line.

"Listen, Agatha," said Miss Cackle. "You must admit that you don't really have much choice. If you will agree to abide by the Witches' Code, then we can change you back, but not otherwise. If you agree, go back into line so that we know what you want us to do."

The snail shuffled back into line again.

Miss Hardbroom spoke the words of the spell which released them, and suddenly the room was full of witches, all looking furious and talking angrily at the same time. The noise was terrible.

"Will you be quiet at once!" commanded Miss Cackle.

She turned to Mildred who was still perched on her chair. "You may go back to bed, Mildred, and in view of what you have done for the school this morning, I think we will have to forget about the interview you were to have had with Miss Hardbroom and myself this afternoon. Don't you agree, Miss Hardbroom?"

Miss Hardbroom raised one eyebrow and Mildred's heart sank.

"Before I agree, Miss Cackle, if you'll forgive me," she said, "I would just like to ask Mildred what she was doing wandering about on the mountain when she should have been in bed?"

"I—I was out for a walk, Miss Hardbroom," replied Mildred.

"And you just happened to have your spell book with you."

"Yes," agreed Mildred, unhappily.

"Such devotion to the school!" said Miss Hardbroom, smiling in a most unpleasant way. "Taking your spell book with you wherever you go. I expect you were also singing the school song as you rambled along, weren't you, my dear?"

Mildred looked at the floor. She could feel all the other witches staring at her.

"I think we must let the child go to bed," said Miss Cackle. "Run along now, Mildred."

Mildred shot out of the room before her form mistress could say anything else, and was in bed in five seconds!

# CHAPTER TEN

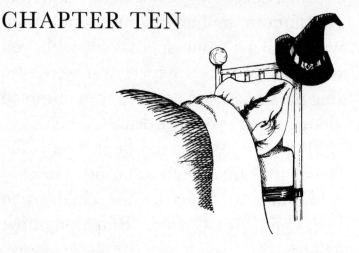

A T NOON the rising bell clanged through the corridors but Mildred pulled the pillow over her head and went back to sleep. It wasn't long before the door of her room burst open.

"Wake up, Mildred!" shrieked Maud, seizing the pillow and hitting her friend over the head with it.

Mildred screwed up her eyes against the daylight and saw what seemed to be hundreds of people around the bed all talking and shouting. Maud was actually *on* the bed, bouncing up and down.

"What's the matter?" asked Mildred, sleepily.

"As if you didn't know!" replied Maud, breathless from bouncing. "The whole school's talking about it."

"About what?" said Mildred, who was still half asleep.

"*Will* you wake up?" shrieked Maud, pulling the bedclothes back. "You saved the whole school from Miss Cackle's wicked sister, that's all!"

Mildred sat bolt-upright.

"So I did!" she exclaimed, and everyone laughed.

"Miss Cackle's called a meeting in the Great Hall," said Dawn and Gloria, two other members of Form One. "You'd better hurry and dress. She'll expect you to be there."

Mildred jumped out of bed and her friends went off to the hall. She was soon ready and ran to join them, shoelaces trailing along the floor as usual.

Maud had saved a place for her, and Mildred was embarrassed to notice that everyone stared as she came into the hall. While they waited for the teachers to arrive, Mildred decided to tell her friend about Ethel.

"Listen," she whispered, leaning towards Maud so that no one could hear. "It wasn't my fault about the display. Ethel cast a spell on the broomstick that she lent me, and I know because she told me. Don't tell anyone else, will you? But I wanted you to know because I don't want you thinking that I was just being clumsy."

"But everyone already knows," said Maud.

"Do they?" exclaimed Mildred. "Who told them?"

"Well, you know what Ethel's like," replied Maud. "She just had to tell someone how clever she'd been, so she told Harriet, and Harriet thought it was a dreadful thing to do, so *she* told everyone else. No one's talking to Ethel now and Miss Hardbroom found out too and was furious with her."

"Shhhhh!" said someone. "They're coming."

Everyone stood up as Miss Cackle came in, followed by Miss Hardbroom and all the other teachers.

"You may sit down, girls," said the headmistress. "As you all know, the school narrowly escaped invasion this morning. Had it not been for a certain young member of the school, we should not be here but would be hopping about, turned into frogs."

The girls laughed.

"No, no, girls! Do not laugh! It would not be at all funny had it happened. However, as it did *not* happen, I proclaim the rest of today a half holiday in honour of Mildred Hubble. Mildred, would you come up here for a moment?"

Mildred went bright red and was pushed to her feet. She stumbled through the rows of chairs, tripping over feet as she went, and clumped across the platform to Miss Cackle's table.

"Now, don't be shy, my dear," said Miss Cackle, beaming. She turned to the school. "Come along, school! Three cheers for our heroine Mildred."

Mildred blushed and twisted her fingers behind her back as the cheers rang out.

It was a relief to "the heroine" when it was all over. As they filed out of the hall, she was thumped on the back and congratulated by everyone — except for Ethel, who gave Mildred the nastiest look you've ever seen.

"Good old Mil!" yelled someone.

"We'll get out of our chanting test, thanks to you," said someone else.

"Thanks for the holiday!"

"Thanks, Mil!" And so on.

Maud flung an arm around her friend.

"You did look embarrassed," she said. "You went ever so red, I could see you from the back of the hall!"

"Oh, *don't*," said Mildred. "Let's go and fetch the kittens and make the most of our holiday."

"One moment," said a chilling voice that they knew so well. The two girls turned to find their form mistress standing behind them. They jumped to attention at once, wondering what they had done, which was a natural reaction whenever Miss Hardbroom spoke.

This time, however, to their amazement, she smiled, a friendly smile not like the usual curl at the corner of the lips.

"I just wanted to say thank you, Mildred," she said. "Run along now, girls, and enjoy your holiday before it's over."

She smiled again and vanished.

The girls just stared at each other.

"Sometimes," said Mildred, "I think she probably isn't as mean as we think she is."

"Perhaps you are right, Mildred," said Miss Hardbroom's voice from behind Mildred's ear, and the two girls jumped in horror!

Mildred grabbed her friend's hand and they hurried away down the corridor out into the misty playground, leaving Miss Hardbroom's laughter echoing from nowhere along the empty passage.

For
Luc
and
Isabelle

# THE WORST WITCH
# STRIKES AGAIN

# CHAPTER ONE

SUMMER HAD arrived at Miss Cackle's Academy for Witches. Not that it made much difference to the grim-looking school, which was perched on a mountain amid swirling mist and pine trees.

On the first morning of term, the members of Form One sat in class looking a dismal sight in their new summer uniform, which was even more dreary than the winter one. It consisted of a black-and-grey-checked short-sleeved dress, brightened a little by the sash around the waist, and grey ankle socks with black lace-up shoes. Everyone's knees were startlingly white after spending the winter swathed in itchy black wool stockings.

Despite this picture of gloom, the room buzzed with laughing voices, and the pupils all sounded very excited to be back, except for Mildred. Worried would be a better word to describe how Mildred felt as she sat on her desk listening to Maud's tales of what had happened during the holidays.

In fact, she wasn't really listening to Maud at all because she was busy imagining all the dreadful things that were just bound to happen during the coming term. Why, it hadn't even started yet. There were weeks and weeks to get through! After the appalling report she'd had at the end of last term, she had promised everyone at home that she really would try this term.

Even though Miss Cackle had kindly

mentioned the day when she had saved the school from disaster, it hardly made up for all the days when everything she touched fell to bits or broke or, worse, when she couldn't resist doing something wicked to liven things up a bit. It was the worst report she'd ever taken home.

"Mildred!" Maud broke into her thoughts. "You haven't been listening to a word, have you?"

"Yes, I have," said Mildred.

"Well, what did I say then?" asked Maud.

"Er—you got a pet bat for your birthday?" replied Mildred, hopefully.

"I told you you weren't listening!" cried Maud triumphantly. "That was about ten minutes ago."

The door crashed open and Miss Hardbroom, their terrifying form mistress, swept in like an icy blast, bringing with her a girl whom no one had ever seen before. As usual, everyone nearly jumped

out of their skins, and there was a mad
scramble as desk lids slammed and people
crashed into each other in their hurry to
be standing by their desks in an orderly
manner.

"Good morning, girls," said Miss Hardbroom crisply.

94

"Good morning, Miss Hardbroom," replied the girls.

"I hope you're all glad to be back with us," said Miss Hardbroom, narrowing her eyes and glaring at the unfortunate pupils in the front row. "All nice and rested and looking forward to some hard work?"

"Yes, Miss Hardbroom," chorused the girls in their most sincere voices.

"Good!" said Miss Hardbroom, clapping her hands together in a businesslike way. "Now then. This is Enid Nightshade." She extended a bony hand towards the newcomer, who stood with hunched shoulders, looking fixedly at the floor.

Enid was a tall girl, even taller than Mildred, but much more ungainly, with big hands and feet. There seemed to be an awful lot of her, though she wasn't exactly fat. Her hair was the colour of milky tea and was restrained into a long, thick plait, but you could tell that it would be very

wild and wavy once it was unleashed from the black hair ribbon.

"Enid is newly with us this term," said Miss Hardbroom. "Mildred, Enid is to be entrusted to your care. I must point out that this is not my idea, but some strange notion of Miss Cackle's that if you are awarded such a responsibility it may actually turn you into a responsible member of the community. Personally, I feel it a great loss to send young Enid off down the path of ill-fame with you, when we could all breathe easily if someone like Ethel were to show her the ropes."

Ethel, the form sneak and goody-goody, smiled demurely at this point and everyone felt like hitting her.

"However," continued Miss Hardbroom, "perhaps I shall be proved wrong. I certainly hope so. Please make sure that Enid knows where everything is, Mildred, and keep her company for the next few days. Thank you. Now, Enid, take the desk next to Mildred and let us begin the lesson. The first school assembly will be tomorrow morning in the Great Hall."

"Crumbs," thought Mildred, sneaking a look at Enid, who had crammed her huge frame into the neighbouring desk. "We won't get much fun out of her."

But Mildred couldn't have been more wrong.

# CHAPTER TWO

ARLY next morning before the
rising-bell had rung, Maud crept
along the stone corridor to Mildred's
room and knocked on the door.

There was no reply, but this was hardly
surprising as Mildred was renowned for
her ability to sleep through any amount of
noise; in fact Maud often had to go and
shriek in her friend's ear to waken her
when the rising-bell failed to do so.

Maud tiptoed into the room, closing the
heavy door quietly behind her. Mildred's

three bats skimmed over her head, returning from their night out, and settled upside down on the picture rail.

A soft "miaaow" at her feet reminded Maud of Mildred's little tabby cat, which was threading itself round her ankles. She bent down and picked up the little creature, which immediately draped itself around her neck like a fur stole and began to purr. Maud was quite glad of the warmth, as she felt a bit chilly in her summer night-dress of grey cotton.

"Mildred," she whispered to the bundle of bedclothes. "Wake up, Mildred. It's Maud."

"Whassat?" mumbled Mildred's voice from deep under the covers, followed by a series of rhythmic snores.

"Mildred!" whispered Maud, giving the lump under the covers a vigorous shake. "Wake up!"

The top of Mildred's head appeared on the pillow.

"Oh, hello, Maud!" she said. "Is it time to get up yet? Did I miss the bell?"

"No," said Maud, curling up on the end of the bed. "It's still early. The bats have only just come in. I came to have a chat before the others get up."

Mildred hauled herself into a sitting position.

"Wrap yourself up—you must be freezing," she said, offering Maud her black cloak. Maud took the cloak from the bedpost and put it around her shoulders.

"Thanks," she said. "What shall we do at break?"

"Well," said Mildred, "I've got to show Enid round the school. You know, the potion lab and gym, that sort of thing."

"Can't you hand her over to someone else?" asked Maud, sounding a little touchy. "She looks very dull, and anyway you and I always go about together."

"It's a bit difficult to get rid of her," said Mildred. "Miss Hardbroom asked me, and she'd go berserk if I tried to get out of it. Anyway, the poor girl is new. I feel a bit sorry for her."

"Oh, all right," agreed Maud reluctantly. "I'll come and call for you later and we can at least go to Assembly together."

"Er—well, I'll have to take Enid to

Assembly," said Mildred awkwardly. "But you can come too, though."

"Oh, thanks!" stormed Maud. "I'd rather go on my own." She flung off the cloak and uncurled the cat. "Perhaps you could fit me in later in the week!"

"Oh, Maud!" said Mildred. "Don't be so silly. I didn't mean—"

But Maud had already swept out of the door, letting it bang behind her.

# CHAPTER THREE

**T**EN MINUTES later, the rising-bell clanged and echoed through the corridors. Mildred, who was just on the verge of going back to sleep, steeled herself to get out of bed and grope around for her clothes, which were festooned all over the room as usual. The summer dress was much easier to cope with than the winter uniform. Somehow, in winter she always got in a dreadful muddle with her tie.

She was just about to go and bang on Maud's door and surprise her by being ready when she remembered about Enid and set off to the next corridor to call for her.

"Enid! Are you up yet?" she called softly through the door.

"Hang on a sec!" called Enid's voice. "I'm just feeding the monkey."

"Monkey?" thought Mildred. "I must have misheard."

But she hadn't. When she pushed open the door, there sat Enid on her narrow bedstead. Perched on her shoulder was a slender grey monkey eating a banana.

"It's to go on the back of my broom," explained Enid, as Mildred hastened inside and closed the door, in case by some mischance Miss Hardbroom should materialize outside.

"But it's a *monkey*, Enid!" exclaimed Mildred. "You won't be allowed. It says in the rules that we can only have cats. We can't even have owls."

"Oh, it'll be all right," said Enid airily. "No one'll notice when it's all hunched up on the end of my broom."

"I wouldn't be too sure," said Mildred darkly. "You don't know Miss Hardbroom yet."

"Anyway," continued Enid as if she hadn't heard Mildred's dire warning, "it's much more fun than a silly old cat. It can hang upside down by its tail and do all sorts of things."

"Well," said Mildred doubtfully, "I do hope it'll be all right. Come on, we'd better go down to Assembly or we'll be late, and that would never do when I'm supposed to be looking after you!"

As the girls filed into the Great Hall, Mildred caught Maud by the arm and whispered, "Hey, Maud! You'll never guess what Enid has got in her room."

But Maud didn't answer and brushed past with her nose in the air.

Miss Hardbroom stood beside the headmistress, Miss Cackle, on the platform at
the end of the Great Hall. Unlike Miss
Hardbroom, who was scowling, Miss
Cackle beamed down at her flock, which
stood in neat black-and-grey-checked rows
in front of her. Mildred could not suppress
a snigger at the strange-looking pair they

made. Miss Cackle, short and wearing a tight dress of grey satin which made her look very bulgy, and Miss Hardbroom, tall and extremely thin, wearing a gown with black vertical stripes which made her look even taller.

Miss Hardbroom's piercing gaze swept past like a searchlight, causing Mildred's smile to vanish instantly like the sun behind a cloud.

"Welcome back, girls," said Miss Cackle. "You have a term of hard work ahead of you. As well as the usual exams, there will be the school Sports Day, which I know you all look forward to."

At this point Miss Hardbroom closed her eyes and a look of pain flashed across her face. Mildred also felt a twinge of dread as she remembered the disastrous broomstick display at Hallowe'en the year before.

Now Miss Cackle looked a little shy. "And

there will be my birthday celebration, when I look forward to the little songs and chants which you always prepare for me."

A gentle groan ran round the room. Miss Cackle's birthday celebration was the most boring event of the year.

# CHAPTER FOUR

**A**FTER Assembly the girls marched to the music room for their chanting lesson with Miss Bat, the chanting mistress. She was tiny, thin, and very old, with frizzy grey hair which she wore in a plait twisted around the back of her head. Because of her habit of pressing her jaw into her chest, she had three chins, and this looked very odd on top of her thin little figure. She wore circular steel glasses attached to a chain round her neck (not the dainty gold kind but more like a bicycle chain)

and she always had a conductor's baton tucked behind her ear.

She sat at the piano in a black dress with grey flowers and played a rousing march as the girls entered.

"Chanting's ever so dull," whispered Mildred to Enid as they marched into the music room.

"Don't you believe it," Enid whispered back with a surprisingly wicked glint in her eye.

They all took their places, and Mildred managed to position herself with Maud on one side and Enid on the other, though Maud still looked very crotchety and wouldn't return Mildred's smile.

Miss Bat struck up the opening chord to a chant that they all knew very well, and the girls began.

To Mildred's surprise, Enid was singing completely out of tune — not loud enough for Miss Bat to hear, but loud enough so that Mildred couldn't concentrate on the right note herself. Verse after verse droned on with Enid just missing the correct note and the pupils around her struggling to keep in tune.

Mildred sneaked a look at Enid, who was smiling sweetly and obviously doing it on purpose, then glanced at Maud who was trying desperately to keep a straight face. A sudden mad burst of uncontrollable

laughter welled up in Mildred. She clenched her teeth and racked her brains to think of something sad, but the sound of Enid's voice droning flatly on beside her was too much, and a loud snorting noise erupted from Mildred's nose like a motorbike starting up.

Mildred put her hands across her mouth and even tried stuffing her handkerchief into it, but it was no use: a real fit of the giggles was upon her and she just doubled up with helpless laughter and giggled till her face ached.

"Mildred Hubble!" The inevitable words rang out across the room in a tone which implied that Miss Bat would stand no more nonsense. Everyone had stopped chanting, and Mildred's peals of laughter echoed embarrassingly round the silent walls.

"Come out here at once!" ordered Miss Bat.

Mildred clumped through the rows of

pupils and stood next to the piano. She took a deep breath and managed to look serious, though her face was flaming and the sound of Enid's voice still resounded in her head.

When Miss Bat was angry there were two things she always did. First, her head would begin nodding (which it was doing now) and, secondly, she would take the baton from behind her ear and begin conducting an invisible orchestra (which she was also doing now). Mildred could tell that she was furious.

"What, may I ask, is so hilarious that you are prepared to disrupt the entire chanting lesson for the sake of it?" inquired Miss Bat coldly. "No one else seems to be laughing. Perhaps you would let us all in on the joke!"

Mildred stole a glance at Maud and Enid. Maud was staring intently at her feet, and Enid was gazing at the ceiling, the picture of innocence.

"It was—" began Mildred, but a splutter of laughter came out and she dissolved into a giggling wreck again.

At last the wave subsided and she was left breathless, but able to speak.

"*Now*, Mildred," quavered Miss Bat, in a voice like a taut violin string, "I'm waiting for a reasonable explanation."

"Enid was singing out of tune," said Mildred.

"Well!" said Miss Bat. "I hardly think that is a reason for such a display of appalling manners. Come here, Enid my dear."

Enid came and stood next to Mildred by the piano.

"Now, my dear," said Miss Bat kindly, "you must not feel shy because you can't sing very well. I hope you are not too upset just because Mildred decided to make a spectacle of herself on your account. Now, let me hear you sing one or two bars of 'Eye of Toad' and we shall see if we can help you along a little."

Enid obliged in the same wavering, off-key voice as before,

*"Eye of toad,*
*Ear of bat,*
*Leg of frog,*
*Tail of cat.*
*Drop them in,*
*Stir it up,*
*Pour it in a silver cup."*

This was the last straw for Mildred, who abandoned all efforts at keeping control and gave herself up to complete hysteria.

As you may imagine, it was also the last straw for Miss Bat, and Mildred found herself on her way to the headmistress's office for the first time that term.

# CHAPTER FIVE

MISS CACKLE was not pleased when Mildred entered her study.

"Good morning, Mildred," she said wearily, motioning the hapless pupil to sit down. "I suppose it is too much to hope for that you are sent here with a message, or for some innocent reason?"

"Yes, Miss Cackle," murmured Mildred. "Miss Bat sent me to you because I was laughing in the chanting lesson. One of my friends was singing out of tune and I couldn't stop laughing."

Miss Cackle looked at Mildred over the top of her spectacles and Mildred wondered why Enid's singing didn't sound in the least bit funny now, in front of the headmistress.

"I wonder," said Miss Cackle, "if there is any hope at all for you in this Academy. You take one pace forward then four paces backward; it's the same old story, Mildred, isn't it? And the term's only just begun. I see that Miss Hardbroom was right when she disagreed with my plan to put you in charge of the new girl. I have put you in a position of responsibility, Mildred, and you must live up to it, not let me down."

"Yes, Miss Cackle," agreed Mildred fervently.

"It would be a sad thing indeed," continued Miss Cackle, "if you were to lead this innocent new pupil up the garden path with you, would it not? Now, child, for the last time, pull yourself together and let me hear no more about you for the rest of the term."

Mildred assured Miss Cackle of her good intentions and meekly left the room.

As there was still a good hour of chanting left and Miss Bat had told her not to come back, Mildred decided to sneak up to Enid's room and take a look at the monkey.

Mildred could hear her fellow pupils chanting in the music room as she crept up the spiral staircase to Enid's room. It gave her a delicious sense of freedom to have a whole hour stretched before her while everyone else in the school was imprisoned in a stuffy classroom.

For once the sun had filtered through the shroud of mist, and shafts of sunlight fell dramatically through the slit windows onto the cool stone steps.

"Well, I certainly made a mistake about Enid," thought Mildred. "She's worse than I am."

She giggled again at the thought of the
tuneless chanting and opened the door of
Enid's room.

As she did so, the monkey, which had
been sitting on the bedpost, made a dive

for the door straight over Mildred's head
and off down the corridor, screeching
with delight. Mildred saw its long tail
whip round the corner as it plunged down
the spiral staircase.

"Oh, no!" thought Mildred, setting off
after the creature as fast as she could.

She arrived breathless at the bottom of
the staircase, only to find that the monkey
was nowhere to be seen.

"Oh, dear," she muttered aloud. "What *am* I going to do?"

"What *should* you be doing, Mildred?" asked a chilling voice behind her.

"Oh! Er—nothing, Miss Hardbroom," replied Mildred, for it was her form mistress who had appeared from nowhere.

"Nothing," echoed Miss Hardbroom frostily. "At this time of day? Why, I ask myself, should Mildred Hubble be hurtling around the corridors when everyone else is usefully employed in a lesson somewhere?

And why, I ask myself, should Mildred Hubble's socks be trailing round her ankles?"

Mildred bent down and hastily pulled them up.

"I was sent out of chanting, Miss Hardbroom," she explained. "Miss Bat told me not to come back, so I've got nothing to do for the next hour."

*"Nothing to do?"* exploded Miss Hardbroom, her eyes flashing so wildly that Mildred backed away. "Well, I would suggest that you take yourself to the library and brush up on your spells and potions

for a start, and then perhaps if there is any time left—which I doubt—you can come and find me in my room and I will give you a test on what you have learned."

"Yes, Miss Hardbroom," said Mildred.

Desperately trying to work out where the monkey could have got to, Mildred took the corridor which led towards the library. She looked back over her shoulder and saw that Miss Hardbroom had vanished, which was very confusing, as you were never sure if she was watching, invisible, or if she had walked away.

Mildred walked on for a few more corridors, then waited and listened. All she could hear was the faint chanting of Form One in the distance, so she set off in search of the lost monkey again.

Something moving caught her eye through one of the windows. It was the monkey, halfway up one of the towers, swinging about by its tail. It had managed

to get hold of a hat from somewhere and was wearing it rammed down over its ears. If Mildred hadn't been quite so horrified she would have seen how funny the animal looked.

"Oh, come down, Monkey, please!" she called as softly as possible. "I've got a nice banana for you."

But the monkey only let out a shriek and climbed a bit higher. Mildred ran as fast as she could and fetched her broomstick. As far as she could see, the only way to get the monkey down was to fly across and catch it.

Nervously she stepped onto the window ledge and lowered herself onto the broomstick. She gave the command for it to fly, but unfortunately, as she gave it a tap (which was the signal for it to start), she slipped, and the broom zoomed off with Mildred hanging on by her arms.

"Stop!" yelled Mildred, at which the broom stopped and hovered in midair. Mildred tried to haul herself onto it, but that was impossible with nothing to push her feet against. Her arms were practically out of their sockets, but she was so near the monkey that she decided to give it a try and commanded the stick to fly on. As luck would have it, the monkey was

fascinated by the sight of the broom and jumped onto it, where it proceeded to run up and down and swing by its tail.

"Down!" Mildred commanded the broom, and the extraordinary little group whooshed downwards.

As they came in to land, Mildred was shocked to see that the yard was full of people. Form Three had been having a broomstick lesson with Miss Drill, the gym mistress, and had witnessed the whole episode on the tower. Even worse, Miss Hardbroom was standing next to Miss Drill with her arms folded and both eyebrows raised. Mildred felt quite ridiculous as she floated to the ground in such an ungainly position with the monkey swinging beside her.

"Well?" asked Miss Hardbroom, as Mildred took the monkey from the broom and stood holding it tightly in case it should escape.

"I—er—I found it!" exclaimed Mildred.

"On the tower," sneered Miss Hard-broom, "wearing a hat."

"Yes," said Mildred, almost dying of

embarrassment. "It was up there, so I . . . thought I ought to bring it down."

"And where did it come from?" demanded Miss Hardbroom, narrowing her eyes. "You haven't been arguing with Ethel again, have you?" (She was thinking of the time last term when Mildred had changed Ethel into a pig during an argument.)

"No, Miss Hardbroom!" said Mildred.

"Well, then, Mildred, where did you get the monkey from?"

This was a very tricky situation. Mildred could not possibly sneak on Enid but Miss Hardbroom's terrifying stare made Mildred feel that she probably knew anyway. Perhaps it was just as well that a member of Form Three stepped forward.

"She got it from the new girl's room," announced the girl. "I saw her coming out of there earlier on."

"Enid's room?" queried Miss Hardbroom. "But Enid has a regulation black cat. There is no other animal in her room."

She sent the girl to fetch Enid from the chanting lesson and Enid soon arrived looking bewildered. She did not flinch when she saw Mildred with the monkey.

"Is this your monkey, Enid?" asked Miss Hardbroom.

"I only have a cat, Miss Hardbroom," replied Enid.

Mildred's eyes widened in disbelief.

"Are you *quite* sure it isn't Ethel?" asked Miss Hardbroom severely.

"Yes, Miss Hardbroom," said Mildred. Miss Hardbroom, however, did not believe her, and she muttered the spell which would change the animal back to its original form. To Mildred's surprise the monkey vanished and in its place stood a little black cat.

"That's my cat!" cried Enid, as the cat jumped into her arms.

"Mildred!" said Miss Hardbroom. "You've been told about this before. First Ethel, now Enid's cat. For goodness' sake, when is this nonsense going to stop?"

Mildred was astonished.

"But Miss—I—" she gasped.

"Silence," said Miss Hardbroom. "Two days you have been back at school and already twice in disgrace. At least this encounter has allowed Enid to see what a bad example you are. I hope you will take care not to follow in Mildred's footsteps, Enid. Now run along, both of you, and take care, Mildred. Just think before you embark on such an escapade again."

The minute the two girls were round the corner, Mildred asked Enid what on earth was going on.

"Simple," said Enid. "It really is my cat.

I changed it into a monkey before breakfast this morning, for fun. I was going to change it back tomorrow when we go for Sports Day practice. I didn't know you were going to go and let it out, did I?"

# CHAPTER SIX

PORTS DAY loomed ahead like a black cloud for Mildred, as did anything where competition was called for. She hated the idea of trying to beat other people, mainly because she never won and it was all so humiliating, but also because it just wasn't her way of doing things.

As well as this, Maud was being very trying. Just because Mildred had been put in charge of Enid, which meant that she *had* to take Enid around with her, Maud had gone off in a jealous huff and had even gone as far as teaming up with Ethel.

Mildred could hardly believe it when she saw the two of them together. She knew Maud was just doing it because of Enid, so she pretended not to take any notice, but in fact it nearly killed her to see her best friend arm-in-arm with her old enemy.

There were various events on the Sports Day agenda: pole vaulting, sack racing, cat balancing, relay broomstick racing, and a prize for the best-trained cat.

Everyone practised very hard in the weeks leading up to Sports Day. Mildred had long sessions with her little tabby cat,

trying to teach it to sit up straight instead of hanging on with its eyes shut, but little progress was made. Mildred and Enid ran races against each other and always tied, but this was no indication of merit, as they were equally bad.

The weeks soon slid by and Sports Day dawned grey and misty. For once Mildred was wide awake when the rising-bell sounded, as she had been tossing and turning for most of the night with dreadful nightmares. One was about finding a monster on the back of her broom in the middle of the relay race, and it turned into Miss Cackle who said, "Mildred! You've done it again!"

As the first peals of the bell rang out, Mildred dragged herself out of bed and rummaged around for her sports kit. She found it crumpled up at the bottom of her sock drawer and tried to smooth it out so it would look a bit more presentable.

Some mornings were worse than others, she reflected as she pulled on the dingy grey aertex shirt and black divided skirt which hung limply to her knees. The grey socks and black plimsolls completed the picture of gloom as she plaited her hair tightly.

There was a knock at the door and for a happy moment she thought it must be Maud, but Enid put her head round the door and Mildred remembered Maud had gone off with Ethel.

"Don't laugh," said Enid as she brought the rest of herself into the room.

Mildred obliged with a snort of mirth at the sight of Enid's sports kit.

"I said *don't* laugh," said Enid, smiling. "I know they're funny, but I haven't got a proper pair."

She was wearing a vast pair of black knickers which were pulled up under her arms.

"Haven't you got a smaller pair?" asked
Mildred.

"No," replied Enid. "My mother buys
everything with growing room because
I'm so big. You should see my vests! Some

of them trail on the floor when they aren't tucked in."

"I shan't be able to keep a straight face with you in those," said Mildred. "Still, it might put the others off. How's your cat?"

"I'm not bringing it," said Enid. "It's been a bit off-colour since the monkey incident. I don't think it could cope with broomstick riding."

"I'm bringing Tabby," said Mildred, taking the cat from its position curled up on the pillow. "I've been training it every day, but I don't know if it's done any good."

# CHAPTER SEVEN

**E**NID AND Mildred sat in the cloak-room to be called for the first event, which was the pole vault. To their great consternation they discovered that they had been entered for everything, mainly because they were both so tall, and this gave rise to the completely false idea that they must be good at sports.

"We're *bound* to come last," said Enid despairingly.

"We don't have to," said Mildred, stroking the tabby cat's head, which was sticking out of the top of her shoe bag.

"We're taller than everyone else—we *ought* to be better than them."

*"Exactly,"* said Enid miserably. "But we aren't. What we need is a touch of magic."

"Oh, Enid," said Mildred anxiously. "I can't even do that properly. You weren't here when I made the wrong potion in the potion lab and Maud and I disappeared. It was dreadful."

"Leave it to me," said Enid with disarming confidence.

Mildred watched as her friend took the two poles to the window and waved her arms around them, muttering words under her breath.

"What are you doing?" asked Mildred.

"Shhh," said Enid. "You'll mess up the spell."

A minute later, Enid handed Mildred's pole back to her. . . .

"Come on," she said. "We'll beat the lot of them now."

Mildred felt distinctly uneasy as they joined the contestants for the pole vault. She looked up at the bar, which seemed to be at least a mile high.

"I'll never get over that," she whispered to Enid.

"Mildred Hubble!" announced Miss Drill.

"Oh, no!" gasped Mildred. "I'm first."

"Just jump," said Enid with a wink. "You'll be all right."

So Mildred jumped. She charged along the run-up strip, banged the pole onto the ground, and as she did so, an extraordinary thing happened. The ground suddenly seemed to be made of a strong, springy material, and both Mildred and the pole went soaring up into the air.

From somewhere far below she heard Enid shout, "Let go of the pole!"

Glancing down, Mildred saw to her horror that everything was way below

her, including the pole vault bar and the
school walls. She was so shocked that she
hung on even more tightly and saw that
a turret was looming up in front of her
with gathering speed. Like a guided mis-
sile, Mildred and the pole shot straight
through one of the windows (fortunately

the castle-like school did not have glass in any of them) and crash-landed in the middle of a table all set out ready for somebody's tea.

Lying dazed on the floor amid shattered teacups and pools of milk, Mildred saw to her dismay that she had hurled herself into Miss Hardbroom's private

study. The pole was neatly broken in two with one half embedded in a portrait of Miss Hardbroom, and the other half in the cat basket, having just missed Miss Hardbroom's cat, now snarling and spitting on top of a cupboard.

It wasn't very long before the door opened and Miss Hardbroom, Miss Cackle, and Miss Drill all came bursting in through the door. The terrified cat leapt onto its owner's shoulders with a yowl.

"Nice of you to drop in, Mildred," sneered Miss Hardbroom. "However, it was hardly necessary to use such an

unorthodox method of getting here. Everyone else seems to find the stairs perfectly adequate."

"I'm sure I do not have to remind you, Mildred," said Miss Drill, "that it is against the rules to use magic in any sporting event."

"I just cannot understand it," sighed Miss Cackle, removing a squashed jam tart from Mildred's hair and absentmindedly feeding it to Miss Hardbroom's cat. "I can hardly believe that one of my girls would cheat, and that poor new girl witnessing such an example. Shocking, shocking."

Mildred silently ground her teeth when she thought of the number of times "the poor new girl" had got her into trouble since term began.

"This *must* be positively the last time that anything of this sort happens," said Miss Cackle sternly. "You are disqualified from the rest of the events, and if I see you in trouble even once more this term then I shall have to disqualify you from the school itself."

Mildred gasped.

"Yes, Mildred," Miss Cackle continued, "I shall be forced to expel you if this reckless behaviour continues. Now go to your room for the rest of the day and ponder upon all I have told you."

Mildred was only too glad to escape to her room. She curled up on her bed with the little cat and listened to the rest of the school laughing and cheering outside as Sports Day continued.

"It's impossible, Tabby," she said. "I shall never get right through to the end of term without *anything* happening."

There was a tap at the door and in came Enid.

"What happened?" she asked. "Where did you land?"

"Oh, it was awful!" said Mildred. "I ended up in Miss Hardbroom's study. Miss Cackle said she'll expel me if I do anything else this term. What about you? Did you go too high as well?"

"Oh, no," said Enid. "I realized that I must have over-magicked the poles, so I pretended to faint and got sent off to the restroom. I'll have to nip back in a minute. Did you get hurt?"

"Not much," said Mildred ruefully. "Just twisted my ankle a bit. I'm all right."

"Well, cheer up," said Enid brightly, opening the door. "At least nothing else can go wrong today. I'll see you later."

Mildred managed a weak smile as Enid disappeared into the corridor.

"Oh, Tabby," she said miserably to the little cat. "We've got one more chance — that's all."

# CHAPTER EIGHT

**M**ILDRED had not felt so anxious about being expelled since the day when she had ruined the broomstick formation team at Hallowe'en. She remembered all the promises to her family about being good, and thought how dreadful it would be if she arrived home with her cat and suitcases to break the dreadful news to them. She looked at her calendar and decided to struggle through each day as it came, making every effort to reach the end of term without any more incidents.

Enid tried to tempt her to every imaginable escapade during the weeks that followed, but with admirable strength of mind Mildred resisted. Ethel was being particularly provoking because Maud was still her friend, but Mildred withstood all teasing and managed to battle through to the last week of term without any more trouble at all.

Miss Cackle's birthday celebration was to be held as usual on the last day of term, and each class had chosen a little chant or poem to be performed on the day. Maud had been chosen to represent Form One and Mildred was relieved not to be involved apart from having to sit and listen.

"This is going to be awful," announced Enid as they sat in class waiting to be called to the Great Hall. "Why don't we skip it? I don't know if I can stand a whole morning of recitation."

"No," replied Mildred flatly.

"Oh, go on, Mil," said Enid persuasively. "You aren't any fun anymore. No one is going to see if we sneak off. The whole school's there. No one will notice if *we* aren't."

"They will, and I'm not," said Mildred. "I've only got another three or four hours to get through, then I can go home for the holidays without being expelled. I just can't risk it."

"Oh, all right," agreed Enid, sounding very disgruntled.

Miss Hardbroom appeared in the doorway and signalled the class to march down to the Great Hall. As they filed down the corridor, Enid suddenly grabbed Mildred's arm.

"Quick!" she hissed. "In here!"

They were passing a store cupboard at the time, and before Mildred knew what had happened Enid had dived inside, pulling Mildred with her.

"What on earth are you doing?" whispered Mildred as Enid hastily closed the door.

"Shhh," said Enid. "All we have to do is to stay in here till they're all in the Assembly Hall, then we can go off and spend the morning as we like."

"But—oh, Enid!" said Mildred hopelessly. "We're bound to get caught."

Meanwhile, outside, Ethel's eagle eye had seen Mildred and Enid vanishing into the cupboard; so had Maud, who secretly wished she had been with them. Life had

been such fun with Mildred as her best friend, and a whole term in Ethel's company had been very unpleasant indeed, especially as Ethel *would* keep going on about how dreadful Mildred was.

As Maud and Ethel passed by the cupboard, Ethel turned the key and locked the door.

"Ethel!" said Maud as they marched on into the Assembly Hall. "That was mean. You'll get them into trouble. Miss Cackle said she'd expel Mildred if she did anything else."

"Exactly," said Ethel triumphantly.

"I think you're a beast," said Maud. "I'm going to creep back and let them out."

But at that moment Miss Hardbroom swept along the corridor and escorted Maud's section of the line into the hall, so there was no way in which she could get back to unlock the cupboard door.

Inside the cupboard, the two young witches heard the key turn.

"I knew it," said Mildred. "We can't get out now and it's the last day of term. We'll have to bang on the door when they all come out of the hall or we'll be in here for the whole of the holiday. They'll open the door at the beginning of next term and all they'll find will be a little heap of bones."

Mildred burst into tears at this distressing thought.

"Oh, Mil, I am sorry," said Enid. "I'll tell them it's my fault. Don't cry. You won't be expelled, I promise."

# CHAPTER NINE

WHEN THEIR eyes had become accustomed to the dim light in the cupboard, Mildred and Enid looked around and saw that they were in a very large, high-ceilinged room which was obviously used for storing old furniture. The light was filtering in from an arched window high up in one corner.

"We're saved!" shrieked Enid, snapping her fingers. "There's a window. All we have to do is get up there."

"Oh, that's easy," said Mildred sarcastically. "It's only about ten feet up the wall. Why don't we fly?"

"Perhaps we could pile some of these things and climb up," said Enid desperately, rummaging through the old desks, broken benches, and cardboard boxes full of rubbish. "Look, Mildred!" she exclaimed. "It's a broomstick!"

She hauled from a wooden chest an ancient broomstick, almost snapped in two but for a few splinters of wood still holding it together. Enid took off her sash and bound it as tightly as possible.

"There!" she said. "Now we *can* fly up.
The window looks big enough for us both
to squeeze out of. Come on."

They commanded the broomstick to
hover, which it did, and the two worst
witches in the school balanced themselves
on it. Enid sat in front and Mildred hung
on round her waist. They made the broom
rise like a helicopter, which is done by saying, "Up, up, up!" over and over again until
you get as high as you want to go. It is a
very jerky process, and the two witches

found it very hard to stay on, but at last they reached the windowsill.

"What can you see on the other side?" asked Enid, concentrating on keeping the broom steady.

Mildred peered through and saw a long indoor wall and part of a ceiling stretching away before her.

"That's odd," she said to Enid. "It isn't an outside window. It seems to lead into a huge stone room.

"Well, we'd better go through before this broom gives up on us," said Enid, sneezing from the dust and cobwebs draped all over them. "Duck your head as we go through."

"I wonder where we'll come out?" mused Mildred as they flew awkwardly through the window.

# CHAPTER TEN

SILENCE had been called in the Great Hall. Maud, who was the first performer, stood on the stage with Miss Cackle and all the mistresses behind her and the rest of the school facing her in the lower part of the hall. She was so worried about Mildred being locked in the cupboard that she could not remember the beginning of the poem, though she had been rehearsing it for weeks. As she stood there wildly searching her memory, there was a loud sneeze and a strange scuffling sound at the back of the hall, and suddenly from a high window in the far corner Mildred and Enid came sailing out, covered in dust and holding on for dear life. The pupils all turned to look, and the teachers froze.

It took a split second for Maud to realize that she was not imagining things and that the window must face into the cupboard. Quick as a flash she cleared her throat.

"Miss Cackle and staff!" she announced importantly, her voice trembling. "I am proud to announce a surprise item from Mildred Hubble and Enid Nightshade. A double broomstick display on a solo broomstick!"

She waved an arm in the direction of Mildred and Enid, who looked positively thunderstruck when they realized exactly what they had flown into.

"I don't believe it," muttered Mildred, as every pair of eyes in the school turned on the unlucky pair.

"If we manage to get out of this one, we deserve a medal," said Enid.

"Let's at least have a try, and do as Maud said," whispered Mildred. "Hold the broomstick steady and fly about a bit, and I'll do some fancy-work if I can."

Enid started to fly the broom slowly round the hall and Mildred clambered up onto the back of it. Clinging on to Enid's shoulders, she managed to do an extremely wobbly arabesque. In fact she had never even stood up on a broomstick before and was rather pleased with herself. She did one with the other leg, and then got very daring and raised one arm up at the same time. Enid, who was not good at steering at the best of times, was not looking where she was going and saw the chandelier approaching just above her head.

"Mildred!" she exclaimed, but it was too late. Mildred crashed straight into it and Enid flew on, leaving her friend dangling from the vast chandelier by one arm. She turned the broom and came back to pick Mildred up.

"That was a narrow squeak," gasped Mildred, settling onto the broom. "For goodness' sake, watch where you're going!"

"What?" said Enid, turning her head.

"I said watch out!" yelled Mildred as a wall came looming up in front of them.

Enid swerved violently and Mildred fell off, just catching the broom by her fingertips and swinging in the air. At that moment, the long-suffering broomstick began to creak ominously in the middle where the sash was loosening.

"Quick, Enid!" said Mildred in despair. "Take it in to land before it falls to bits!"

Enid guided the broom onto the stage next to Maud, who, with great presence of mind, began applauding, joined heartily by the rest of the school.

Miss Cackle and Miss Hardbroom stepped forward. Miss Cackle had a slightly puzzled expression on her face, but Miss Hardbroom had one eyebrow raised like a dagger.

"Mildred Hubble," she began in her most terrifying tone of voice, but before she could launch into the attack, Miss Cackle put an arm around both Mildred's and Enid's shoulders.

"Thank you, children," she said, smiling shortsightedly through her horn-rimmed spectacles. "Not very well executed, and

the state of your clothing leaves much to be desired, but it was a good try. This is what we like to see in the Academy. Team spirit, initiative, but above all, *effort*."

"Thank you, Miss Cackle," said Mildred and Enid, not daring to look up in case they caught Miss Hardbroom's eye.

Miss Cackle smiled mistily and motioned the girls back to their seats. Of course there weren't any seats for Mildred and Enid, who hadn't been there in the first place, but luckily benches had been used, so Maud squashed up, and Enid and Mildred crammed in next to her.

As they filed out of the hall into the yard to wait for the bell which signalled the end of term, Maud told them about Ethel turning the key and the following events, and suddenly they all saw the funny side of it.

"Thanks, Maud," giggled Mildred.

"It's all right," said Maud awkwardly. "Can we be friends again, Mildred?"

"We already are," said Mildred, feeling a bit embarrassed. "You've just saved us from a fate worse than death. Did you see her face?"

"*Whose* face, Mildred?" asked Miss Hardbroom's voice.

The three girls jumped in alarm as Miss Hardbroom materialized in the doorway.

"I—I was just saying," said Mildred,
"that we didn't do our surprise item very
well and you didn't look too pleased."

"I wasn't," snapped Miss Hardbroom.
"However, I do think that the prize for

initiative should go to Maud here. You have her to thank for saving you from a fate worse than death, whatever that may have been!"

She stood aside and waved a hand towards the sunny yard, and the girls dived gratefully outside.

"She can see through walls," whispered Maud.

"Shhh!" said Enid, glancing round. "She really can."

The bell rang out across the school, telling the pupils that it was time to go and collect their cases. Mildred let out a cry of delight and danced her two friends round in a circle.

"I've done it!" she announced. "It's the last day of term, and I'm not expelled!"

# A BAD SPELL FOR
# THE WORST WITCH

# CHAPTER ONE

T WAS the very first day of Mildred Hubble's second year at Miss Cackle's Academy for Witches.

The school year at the academy was divided into two long terms, the first of these commencing in September and stretching right to the end of January. This was known as the Winter Term and was followed by a month of welcome holiday. The second session began in March and finished at the end of July, and this was called the Summer Term, though in fact it was still extremely cold and wintry when term began. Then there was another glorious month of holiday until the beginning of September, and the start of another year.

After her disastrous first year at the academy, it was something of a miracle that Mildred was returning there at all. She was one of those unfortunate people who seem to invite disaster wherever they go. Despite her efforts to be helpful and well behaved, Mildred had an uncanny knack of appearing to be the cause of any trouble which was occurring, and it must be admitted that there *were* occasions (particularly when her rather wild imagination ran away with her) when she managed to turn some peaceful event into a scene of total chaos.

However, *this* year Mildred was older and hopefully wiser (at any rate she was more full of good intentions than ever) and she was quite determined to lose

her reputation as the worst witch in the school.

Arriving on her broomstick at the prisonlike school gates, Mildred peered through the railings into the misty playground. For once she was early and there were only a handful of girls in the yard, all stamping their feet and huddling in their cloaks to keep out the bitter cold. It was always chilly at the school because the building was made of stone, rather like a castle, and was perched on the topmost peak of a mountain, surrounded by

pine trees which grew so close together that it was very damp and gloomy. In fact, the girls suffered permanently from colds and flu from all the time they were forced to spend in the freezing playground.

"Healthy fresh air!" Miss Drill, the gym mistress, would bark, herding the sneezing, coughing pupils outside. "It'll do you all a power of good. Five hundred lines to anyone caught sneaking in before the bell!"

Mildred flew over the gates and landed expertly on the other side.

"Well, *that's* a good start!" she thought, looking around in the hope that someone had witnessed so successful a landing, but of course they hadn't. People were only ever watching when she did something dreadful, never at a moment of triumph.

Mildred took her suitcase from the back of the broomstick which was hovering politely, waiting for the next command. Then she turned her attention to the tabby cat still spread-eagled on the back of the broom with its eyes screwed tightly shut and its claws gripping on for dear life. The poor little cat had never got over its terror of flying, and Mildred always had to prise it from the broomstick whenever she arrived anywhere.

"Trust *me* to get a cat like you," said Mildred fondly, stroking it with one hand and unclasping its claws with the other. "Come on, silly, we're here. Look! It's all over, you can jump off now."

The cat opened one eye cautiously, saw that it was true, and sprang onto Mildred's shoulder, where it rubbed its head gratefully against her hair. Mildred felt a wave of tenderness towards the scrawny creature.

"Mildred! Millie! It's *me*!" shrieked a familiar voice from above. Mildred looked up and saw Maud swooping over the gates, waving her hat in the air. This last action nearly caused her to fall off and she lurched to a rather drunken halt at Mildred's feet.

"Oh, Maud!" laughed Mildred, full of joy at the sight of her best friend after the long summer holiday. "Gosh, you look a lot thinner, and your hair's got longer."

"I know," said Maud, stroking her hair,

which was in two stubby plaits instead of her usual bunches. "Mother put me on this *awful* diet. I wasn't allowed to eat *anything* except lettuce and celery and dreadful stuff like that. Still, I'm out of her clutches now, so it's back to good old school dinners. Three cheers for date-pudding and custard, I say!" They both laughed.

"I don't know why they bother to *have* gates at this school," remarked Mildred, as another three pupils soared over the wall on their brooms.

"Perhaps it's in case we have some

ordinary visitors," said Maud. "You know, people who don't have brooms. Miss Cackle couldn't expect ordinary guests to bring ladders with them, could she? Who else has arrived, by the way? Anyone *we* know?"

"Only Ethel," replied Mildred. "She pretended not to see me though, not that I *care*, of course."

Ethel Hallow was the form sneak and goody-goody, and it was hardly surprising that Mildred felt unfriendly towards her after all the mean tricks Ethel had played during their first two terms, including almost getting Mildred expelled on two occasions.

"Oh, look, Maud!" said Mildred, indicating two small girls in brand-new hats and huge cloaks which nearly touched their brand-new shining boots. "They must be first-years; look at them. Don't they look *little*?"

"To think *we* were like that," said Maud in a motherly way. "It makes me feel quite old."

The two first-years were standing close together, looking lost and shy. One of them was glancing nervously around, and the other was trying unsuccessfully to stop crying. They were a sorry-looking pair. Both were thin; the weeping one had a pinched, pale face and wispy mouse-coloured hair, and the other one had brilliant orange frizzy bunches. For some reason, the weeping one reminded Mildred very strongly of someone else, though she couldn't think who it was.

"Let's go and cheer them up, shall we?" suggested Mildred. "They can't help being new, poor things. Remember how awful *we* felt?"

Feeling very grown-up and wise, Maud and Mildred sauntered casually over to the two pathetic little girls.

"Hello," said Mildred. "You must be new."

"Yes," chorused the girls.

Mildred patted the snivelling one awkwardly on the shoulder. "Don't cry," she said stiffly. "It isn't *that* bad, you know." Unfortunately, Mildred's kindly gesture only served to make matters worse, instead of better, for the girl burst into deafening sobs and flung her arms round Mildred's waist.

Mildred was appalled. Everyone in the playground was staring at her, and any minute now Miss Hardbroom (Mildred's

terrifying form mistress from the previous year) was bound to appear and accuse her of upsetting a poor new girl.

Maud detached the girl rather roughly and gave her a shake. "Stop that silly noise at once!" she said crossly. "You'll get Mildred into trouble before the first bell's even rung."

Mildred smoothed her cloak. "What's your name?" she asked.

"Sybil," snuffled the girl.

"Mine's Clarice," volunteered the other one.

"Are the teachers strict here?" asked Sybil, wiping her eyes with a corner of her voluminous cloak.

"Not really," replied Maud.

"Well, Miss Hardbroom is," said Mildred. "In fact she's the worst of the lot, and she'll be *your* form mistress. We're lucky this year because we'll get Miss Gimlett, and she's quite nice. But Miss *Hardbroom's*

horrendous. She just *appears* out of thin air—" At this point Mildred broke off and looked around in case she had done just that, but she hadn't.

"—*And* she says dreadful things to you in front of the whole class and makes you feel really stupid," continued Maud.

"That's right," said Mildred, "and *I* heard tell that she changed *one* girl into a frog because she was two seconds late for a lesson. I don't know if it's true, but there *is* a frog sometimes seen near the pond in the backyard, and I've heard that it's *really* a poor first-year who—"

"I've never heard that before!" gasped Maud. "*Is* it true?"

"I *think* so," answered Mildred, though in fact she had made up the tale on the spur of the moment and it had somehow got rather out of hand. To be honest, Mildred's stories often got rather out of hand, when she would find, to her dismay, that the whole class was listening and believing every word. She just *couldn't* say then that she'd made it all up.

Poor Sybil believed every word of Mildred's story about the frog and she burst into renewed and even noisier sobs, so deafening that Maud and Mildred thought it best to scurry away, leaving Clarice to offer comfort.

"Mildred! Maudie! Yoo-hoo! It's *me*!"

Enid Nightshade, the new girl who arrived last term and was now their friend, came zooming over the treetops and screeched to a halt so forcefully that

her cat and suitcase shot off the back, and Maud and Mildred had to leap out of the way to avoid being run over.

At that moment the bell rang and the three witches picked up all their belongings and struggled inside with them.

"Thank goodness we haven't got H.B. anymore," whispered Enid. (H.B. was their nickname for Miss Hardbroom.)

"Yes," agreed Mildred. "This year should be as easy as pie without *her* breathing down our necks."

# CHAPTER TWO

HE FIRST announcement made by Miss Cackle at assembly was the ghastly news that Miss Hardbroom had changed places with Miss Gimlett, and would now be accompanying her old form into their second year. An audible groan rippled through the new Form Two, quelled at once by one of Miss Hardbroom's piercing glances, which always made each pupil feel that they had been noticed personally.

With a sinking heart, Mildred moved miserably through all the chores of the first day, unpacking robes, arranging the new books in her desk, feeding the cat, and innumerable small tasks till at last it was bedtime.

The pupils were too depressed to bother sneaking into each other's rooms for a chat as they usually did on the first night back at school. Mildred lay in a glum heap under the blankets with the cat purring like a lawn mower on her pillow, trying to think if there was any possible advantage in another year with Miss Hardbroom at the helm, but there wasn't.

Next morning, Mildred was jolted awake by the bell ringing in a much more frantic way than usual. It didn't take long for the cobwebs of sleep to clear and for her to realize that it was the fire bell.

An untidily dressed Maud flung open Mildred's door as she rushed past. "Quick, Mil!" she shrieked. "It's fire drill, come on!"

"What a time to choose," said Mildred,

bundling on her tunic over her pyjamas. "Perhaps it's a real fire?"

Maud went rushing off down the corridor, but Mildred stopped and looked out of the window to see if there was any evidence of fire. There, in the yard below, was Miss Hardbroom wreathed in thick purple smoke. She appeared to be standing in her customary arms-folded, upright posture, staring into the smoke as if she was in a trance, which seemed decidedly odd, given the circumstances.

"Crumbs!" thought Mildred. "She's gone into a state of shock. I'll have to help!"

Mildred rushed to the washroom and seized the bucket which stood under the window there to catch drips from the leak in the ceiling. It was already half full with stagnant rainwater, so Mildred filled it to the brim, then carried it back to the yard windowsill, collecting her broomstick on the way.

She peered out of the window again, hoping that she might perhaps have imagined the scene below, but Miss Hardbroom had not moved and was now almost hidden from view by the smoke.

"Here goes!" said Mildred, her spirits rising as she thought how grateful her form mistress would be. "Perhaps I'll get a medal for bravery."

It is difficult, at the best of times, to balance on a broomstick, but when you are trying to carry a heavy bucket of water at the same time, it is virtually impossible. Mildred did her best to arrange the bucket hanging from the back, but it was obviously going to spill the minute they took off, so she put the bucket back onto the windowsill, climbed onto the broom first, and then settled the bucket in her lap. This

seemed to be reasonably steady, so taking her courage in both hands, Mildred gave the word: "Down, broom! Fast!"

Instantly they plunged into a vertical nosedive so abrupt that the bucket flew from her grasp and dropped like a stone. Mildred swooped desperately after it but, alas, too late. A torrent of foul, icy water drenched Miss Hardbroom from head to toe, followed a second later by the bucket, which crashed over her head with a doom-laden clang. To give the stern form mistress some credit, it must be recorded that she did not flinch when the metal bucket struck after falling from such a height.

Though her natural inclination was to turn round and zoom straight back again, Mildred could see that there was no escape. The smoke had cleared, revealing at least half the school lined up in rows and Miss Hardbroom still in the same position, with the bucket neatly over her head. For a mad moment, Mildred thought that perhaps, for some unknown reason, it was only a statue of Miss Hardbroom, but this illusion was shattered when the statue spoke.

"There is no need to ask *which* pupil is responsible for this," came the familiar voice from inside the bucket. "Mildred Hubble, perhaps you would be kind enough to assist me in my predicament?"

The sight of any other teacher dripping with water and with a bucket over her head would have been an occasion for great mirth among the pupils, but absolutely nothing could diminish Miss Hardbroom's

power. Not a sound was heard, not a smirk flickered on any face as Mildred stepped forward and stood on tiptoe to remove the bucket.

Miss Hardbroom's eyes bored into Mildred like a laser beam the moment they came into view.

"Thank you, Mildred," she said acidly.

"I—I'm s-sorry, M-M-Miss Hardb-bb-room," gibbered Mildred. "It was—I thought you were on fire—there was smoke so I, well I thought—it seemed . . ."

"Mildred," said Miss Hardbroom heavily, "does it seem likely to you that I would be standing here in the middle of a raging inferno, casually rounding up all you girls?"

"There was the smoke, Miss Hardbroom," explained Mildred in a tiny voice, suddenly feeling aware of the striped pyjama legs under her tunic.

"*If* you remember your fire drill Mildred," said Miss Hardbroom, "pupils are expected in the yard through the main door, and *not*, as some girls seem to imagine, from the upstairs windows. On entering the yard through the *correct* entrance, they would have been met by me, who would then have informed them that the smoke was merely magic smoke to lend atmosphere to the proceedings and that there

was no cause for total panic as some pupils would seem to be prone to."

"Yes, Miss Hardbroom," quavered Mildred. "I'm sorry, Miss Hardbroom."

"Get into line, Mildred," ordered Miss Hardbroom. "Let us just say that we expect this to be your only half-witted jape for the entire term. Ethel? Would you please fetch me a towel and my cloak before I turn into an iceberg?"

"Of course, Miss Hardbroom," said Ethel, smiling demurely at her form mistress, but pulling a horrid face at Mildred as she passed her by.

Mildred lined up next to her two friends, Maud and Enid.

"You are the limit, Mildred," whispered Maud.

"I *know*," said Mildred miserably. "I must have been still asleep or something."

"Actually," said Enid, "it was quite funny really."

At this point all three friends felt an unruly wave of amusement sweeping over them, and the rest of the fire drill was spent desperately avoiding each other's eyes in case a fit of the giggles should descend, and they were all agreed (especially Mildred) that this would definitely *not* be the thing to do.

# CHAPTER THREE

 IRE DRILL was followed immediately by breakfast in the dining hall and everyone was surprised to see Ethel deliberately sitting down next to Mildred, for it was common knowledge that the two were not on the best of terms. "You haven't changed, I see," remarked Ethel provokingly.

Mildred ignored this jibe and sprinkled sugar over her bowl of porridge which resembled a drought-stricken riverbed.

"Actually," continued Ethel, "I've got a bone to pick with you, Mildred Hubble."

"Oh?" said Mildred. "What?"

"It's about terrorizing my little sister," replied Ethel.

"I don't even *know* your little sister!" exclaimed Mildred.

"Really?" said Ethel. "Are you sure you don't remember telling a poor little girl named Sybil some stupid story about being turned into a frog?"

"Gosh, was that your sister?" asked Mildred.

"Yes, it *was*, as a matter of fact," replied Ethel.

"I don't know why we didn't notice, Mil," said Maud, rallying to her friend's side. "We should have noticed that spiky nose anywhere."

Ethel turned deep mauve with rage.

"Oh, come *on*, Ethel," said Mildred, trying to make peace. "It *was* only a made-up story. She *was* being a bit of a weed, and in any case I went to cheer her up in the first place."

"A fine way to cheer people up!" retorted Ethel. "Terrifying the wits out of them. Sybil still hasn't got over the shock, and don't you go insulting my family. Sybil's delicate, not a weed."

"*Look*, Ethel," said Mildred firmly, "just stop it, will you? I'm not getting into a fight over some silly little first-year whether she's your sister or not, and if you'll excuse me, this porridge is bad enough hot, but cold it's inedible and there's a long way to go till lunchtime."

"I won't forget this," muttered Ethel. "No one insults *my* family and gets away with it."

"Weed!" exclaimed Mildred, feeling suddenly reckless after all Ethel's prodding. "All you Hallows are weeds, weeds, weeds!"

Ethel got up and flounced out of the hall, looking grim.

"You shouldn't goad her," said Enid. "You know what she's like."

"I know," said Mildred, "but she does ask for it sometimes with all her airs and graces. No one insults *my* family," she mimicked in Ethel's voice. "She's just an old windbag. She'll have forgotten by tomorrow."

"I wouldn't be too sure about *that*," warned Maud.

After breakfast, Miss Hardbroom announced that the rest of the morning would be devoted to cat training. All the girls were presented with black kittens in their first term at the academy and these were trained to ride on the back of their broomsticks. Mildred, however, had been given a rather dim-witted tabby because there hadn't been quite enough black ones to go round. It seemed rather typical of her luck that she had ended up with the wrong sort of cat, and she couldn't help wondering if Miss Hardbroom had made sure that the misfit kitten had been given to Mildred, rather than to someone like Ethel.

"I hope you have all been practising during the holiday," said Miss Hardbroom, as the girls all lined up with their brooms hovering next to them and the cats perched on the back — that is to say, *most* of the cats were perched on the back. Mildred's tabby

was clinging desperately to the front of her cardigan, its claws hooked in and a wild, desperate look on its face.

"The cat is supposed to be on the broomstick, Mildred," said Miss Hardbroom wearily.

"Yes, Miss Hardbroom," agreed Mildred, dragging the cat from her front and reducing the cardigan to shreds at the same time. The desperate creature immediately spread itself flat on the back of the broom with its eyes glued shut as if awaiting execution.

"How many terms have you been training that cat, Mildred?" said Miss Hardbroom. "Look at the other cats. None of *them* seem to be finding it so terribly difficult to just *sit* on their brooms. It is not as though they were being asked to do an aerobatic display, Mildred. Now take that cat to your room and work with it there for the rest of the morning. The creature is not fit to be seen until it is properly trained. It is a disgrace to the academy."

"Yes, Miss Hardbroom," said Mildred, now faced with the embarrassing task of prising the unfortunate cat from the broomstick and making her way miserably from the yard with the taunting stare of Ethel boring into her back.

Inside her room, Mildred decided to get into bed for a few minutes to warm up. It was a freezing cold day and her feet were like blocks of ice after the session in the yard. The cat, delighted that its ordeal was over, burrowed under the covers like a furry hot-water bottle, and although Mildred had only meant to sit and get warm, within a few minutes her eyelids began to droop, and before long she was fast asleep — *so* fast asleep that she did not hear the door opening very quietly.

# CHAPTER FOUR

THE NOISE of the bedroom door being slammed woke Mildred with a start. She opened her eyes and froze with horror and disbelief at the sight of a vast creature staring down at her with green eyes each as big as a lily pond.

Mildred closed her eyes again, hoping that perhaps it was only a nightmare, but when she sneaked another look, the apparition was still there, and now it began patting gently at Mildred with its gigantic paws.

Terrified, Mildred backed away and crashed into something hard, which seemed to be a huge iron railing towering above her. However, at this distance from the monster, she could see that it was none other than her own tabby cat, which for some reason had grown to the size of a mammoth.

Knowing the cat as well as she did, Mildred could see that, despite its size, it was frightened out of its wits. Her suspicions flew at once to Ethel having cast a spell on the cat to get even with Mildred for the insult to Ethel's family.

"Don't be scared, Tab," she started to say, but much to her surprise, all that came out was a strange hoarse noise sounding rather like "Craark!"

Panic began to grip Mildred as it slowly dawned on her that not only Tabby, but also the bedstead, all the furniture, and even the bats sleeping round the picture

rail were many times larger than usual. This led her to the alarming conclusion that it was not *they* who were bigger, but *she* who was smaller — and a *lot* smaller.

She peered over the edge of the bedstead and saw a cliff of bedcover stretching endlessly to the stone floor. Tabby began purring, which sounded, to the miniature Mildred, like a squadron of aeroplanes taking off.

"Oh, do stop it, Tab. I can't hear myself think!" she tried to say, but once again the words seemed to stick in her throat and come out as a croak.

Mildred decided to get to the chest of drawers, on which stood a small mirror, so that she could see just how small she was. The end of the bedstead was only a few inches away from the drawers, but in her new tiny condition it appeared to be miles. However, to her great surprise, she suddenly felt the impulse to take a flying leap at the huge gap, and landed with the ease of an acrobat on top of the chest.

"How strange," thought Mildred. "I had no idea that I could jump like that!"

She soon discovered why, and it was not a pleasant discovery. Looking back at her from the mirror, with eyes like saucers, was a small, olive-green frog. Mildred turned round, but there was no one behind her. She stretched out her hand and saw a green, damp limb reach out to touch the mirror frog's webbed foot. Mildred

began to cry, and as she lifted her hand to wipe away the tears she watched with horrified fascination as the reflection did the same.

"This is no use at all," Mildred said to herself sternly. "Sitting here crying isn't going to change anything. I must get help."

She jumped back onto the bed and noticed something lying on the pillow. It was a giant-sized clump of weeds—Ethel's way of telling Mildred who had cast the spell and why.

Mildred leapt to the floor and sat there for a moment, reflecting on how nice it was to be able to jump such an amazing distance without getting hurt. It reminded her of the disastrous pole vault on the school sports day, when Enid had cast a spell on Mildred's pole to help her, but had inadvertently overdone the magic and Mildred had sailed through Miss Hardbroom's study window.

However, the ability to jump was the *only* pleasant aspect of Mildred's new condition, and a sudden, hot wave of panic seized her. She felt utterly trapped in her small, cramped frog's body, her knees felt bent in the wrong place and her arms were too short, and it was quite terrifying trying to speak and only being capable of a hoarse croaking sound. There was a large gap beneath Mildred's door, and she decided to set off and find someone to help her. Watched by her baffled cat,

Mildred squeezed through the gap and hopped away down the corridor, convinced that *nothing* could be worse than just sitting helplessly in her room.

As it turned out, she would have done better to have stayed on her pillow, for there she might have been found by Maud or Enid, who would possibly have put two and two together at the curious sight of a cat and frog nestling on the same bed. But outside her room, Mildred was just a common frog who had strayed into the school, where it would be unlikely to occur to anyone (except the wicked person who had done the deed) that it might be a second-year witch under an enchantment.

# CHAPTER FIVE

WITH THE worst possible tim-
ing, Mildred turned the corner
just as Miss Hardbroom strode
through the door leading from
the yard.

"Well, well," she said, bending down
and picking up the little frog, "what have
we here, then?" And without further ado,
she crammed Mildred into her pocket
and marched off.

It was not very pleasant in the pocket.
Mildred felt around in the bumping, musty

darkness and discovered a whistle, a notebook with a rubber band round it, and a voluminous handkerchief.

The next thing she knew, Miss Hardbroom had pulled her out of the pocket and plonked her unceremoniously into a high-sided glass jar. Through the glass she saw that she was on a shelf in the potion laboratory and the tall figure of her form mistress was swirling out of the door.

Mildred felt absolutely dreadful. There appeared to be no way of escaping and even if she *did* escape, she had no idea what to do. She wondered if Ethel would relent and change her back, or whether she might be really wicked enough to leave her as a frog forever. She also wondered if Miss Hardbroom and the class would begin to wonder where she was after a while.

They were wondering where she was at that very moment. Miss Hardbroom had, in fact, been on her way to Mildred's room when she encountered the frog. After leaving the potion laboratory, she soon discovered that Mildred was not in her room and set off to look all over the school, where, of course, she did not find the missing pupil. The class, when questioned, did not know where Mildred was either. It was a mystery.

"Perhaps she's run away?" suggested Enid to Maud as the girls trooped in for dinner. "H.B. was cross with her about the cat."

"I don't think so," said Maud. "She would have taken the cat with her if she'd done that."

"Well, I can't think *where* she is then," shrugged Enid.

"Nor can I," said Maud. "But if you ask *me*, Ethel's got something to do with it. She's got that *look* on. You know, that *I*-know-something-*you*-don't sort of look."

"We'd better keep an eye on her then,"
said Enid.

Meanwhile, in the potion laboratory,
Mildred was desperately trying to overbalance the jar by climbing up the side

and leaning on it. However, she could only get up a little way before she tumbled backwards, as the jar had a heavy glass base which proved impossible to overbalance. After several tries, she gave up and wept a pool of panicky, frustrated tears. All she could do now was to rely on Ethel being merciful (which was not one of Ethel's main qualities). Also, Mildred realized that even if Ethel *was* feeling merciful enough to confess, it was quite possible that no one would realize that Mildred was actually the frog in the jar.

Form Two filed into the potion laboratory after dinner for an hour of spell making. Maud and Enid were still racking their brains as to the whereabouts of their friend, and Mildred felt utterly helpless as they passed by her jar and she heard Maud say, "Perhaps she *has* run away, Enid. I mean, I can't think where else she's gone, and she knows she'll get into the most dreadful trouble if she turns up now without a good excuse."

"I'm *here!*" Mildred tried to shriek, but it only came out as a frenzied croaking.

"That is the noisiest frog I've ever had in this laboratory," snapped Miss Hardbroom with a piercing glance at the jar. Mildred lapsed into silence and fixed her eyes on Maud in the hope that she might be able to send some sort of message through the air like a radio wave to her friend. It almost succeeded.

"Enid," said Maud, as they sorted through the ingredients for an invisibility potion, "I'm sure that frog's staring at me.

It hasn't taken its eyes off our table for the last ten minutes."

"Don't be silly," said Enid, "Frogs don't stare at people."

"Well, that one does," said Maud. "Look!" Enid looked. The little frog was definitely gazing hard in Maud's direction, and when it saw Enid turn to look, it began jumping up and down and croaking like a mad thing.

"Maud," said Miss Hardbroom, "would you please remove that frog from the jar and put it into the box in the cupboard? We do not wish to listen to that noise all afternoon."

"CRAARK!" pleaded Mildred. "CRAARK! CRAAARK! CRAAAARK!" Maud approached the shelf cautiously, reached into the jar, and took Mildred out.

Mildred gave one last, long look into Maud's eyes, but she could see that there was no hope of Maud recognizing a

half-mad frog as her best friend. There was nothing for it but to flee.

Mildred leapt into the air as high as her new, powerful legs would take her, and landed with a soft "splat" on Maud and Enid's bench.

"Don't just *stand* there girls!" bellowed Miss Hardbroom, "Catch the creature!"

The entire class took off in pursuit of the frog as it sprang nimbly from bench to bench. Hands clutched and faces loomed, and suddenly Mildred remembered that the class would be making an invisibility potion. (Miss Hardbroom had told them to study for it after breakfast.) Mildred dived for Ethel's bench, knowing that Ethel would have made the best potion of all, and there it was, dark green and bubbling in the cauldron, with a half-full test tube conveniently spilling a puddle of the liquid onto the bench. Mildred's frog tongue shot out and lapped as much as it could.

"Oh, Miss Hardbroom!" she heard Ethel cry. "The frog's disappeared!"

Mildred heaved a sigh of relief and leapt onto the floor, where she huddled in perfect silence under the bookcase near the door.

"How very strange," mused Miss Hard-broom. "Not only the noisiest, but also the most knowledgeable frog I have ever been privileged to meet."

"I'm sure it was trying to tell me something," whispered Maud to Enid. "Perhaps it knows something about Mildred?"

"What could a *frog* know?" asked Enid.

Maud shrugged her shoulders. "*I* don't know," she replied, "but it was no ordinary frog. I can tell you *that* for certain."

# CHAPTER SIX

COWERING beneath the bookcase, Mildred dared not move in case she had begun to be visible again. (When you have taken an invisibility potion, you reappear very gradually, head first, followed by the rest of the body.)

In fact, being invisible is a very odd sensation indeed. Imagine holding out your leg and feeling it with your invisible hand while being unable actually to see it. For this reason, walking becomes rather a difficult experience, as you can feel your feet moving along but cannot see where they are going. This means that you often find yourself moving in the opposite direction to the one intended, which, of course, is extremely annoying.

Mildred held out her arm to see if it had begun to reappear, but it hadn't. Her patience paid off at last when she heard Miss Hardbroom tell the girls to pack up their books, and after much clattering and bustling, the door closed and the laboratory fell silent.

Mildred hopped out and looked around. As usual, there was a gap of several inches under the door. In fact, it seemed to be a school speciality that none of the doors fitted properly and the windows (most of which were slit windows) had no glass in them at all. The whole school seemed to have been designed with the sole purpose of freezing all the pupils to death.

Mildred squeezed through the gap and

set off as fast as possible along the corridor and down the spiral staircase to the yard. From there she hopped to the pond at the back of the school, for she felt sure that she could hide safely there in the weeds and rushes while she tried to find some solution to her appalling problem.

Sitting on a stone in the middle of the water was the large frog that Mildred had often seen, and which had been the inspiration for the tale which had scared Ethel's sister.

"Craark!" it said, and to Mildred's delight, she found that she could understand what the creature meant. It said, "What on earth's the matter with you? Where's the rest of your body?"

Mildred realized that her head had reappeared, which must have looked rather alarming, bobbing about all over the place with no body attached.

"Don't be afraid," said Mildred. "I've taken an invisibility potion and I'm just coming back into view. You'll be able to see all of me in a moment."

"Where did you get the potion from?" asked the frog, slipping silently from the stone and swimming across to Mildred's head.

"Oh, dear," said Mildred, "it's a long story. I'm not really a frog at all. I'm a second-year witch at the school, and this beastly girl called Ethel Hallow has changed me into a frog, and I was—"

"Good gracious me!" exclaimed the frog. "This is quite amazing! *I'm* not a frog either. I'm a magician. What a wonderful coincidence. I've been here for years, and this is the first conversation I've had with a human for simply ages. How extraordinary! Well, well, well, I can scarcely believe it. Allow me to offer you a nice fly from my store."

"A *fly?*" repeated Mildred.

"Oh, dear," said the frog magician. "Of course, you've only been a frog for a while. A fly, my dear—you know, bzzzzzz. They really are quite delicious once you get used to the idea. I nearly starved at first because I couldn't bear the idea of eating—well— insects and the like, but it's amazing what you can get used to."

Mildred grimaced. "I'm hoping to be changed back before I get used to it," she said (with considerable spirit, bearing in mind how hopeless she felt). "Tell me how you got here in the first place."

"Well, my dear," said the frog magician, settling fatly onto a stone. "It was so long ago that I've almost forgotten. Let me see. . . . Yes, well in those days, of course, the castle was not a school. It was used for meetings and conferences of magicians. We used to have a lovely 'do' in the summer. Like a holiday camp it was, endless teas and lectures and displays of magic all afternoon. Anyway, to cut a long story short, I had an argument—rather like *you* did, by the sound of it—with a fellow magician, and this was the result. Before I could persuade him to change his mind, the summer was over, everyone went home, and I was left behind. I've been here ever since. I must admit I get very glum sometimes." He breathed a huge sigh and gazed into the dark water.

"Why don't you come with *me*?" said Mildred brightly. "I'm going to find my friend Maud, after dark. I know I can make her understand, and then she'll be able to help me. She'll help you, too."

A large tear splashed from the frog

magician's eye. "It's no use," he croaked sadly. "It's got to be a magician who takes off the spell. There aren't any in the school, are there?"

"No, there aren't," said Mildred thoughtfully. "All right, then, I'll go to find Maud by myself, but I'll come back for you as soon as I'm changed back, and I'll get you to a magician somehow. I won't forget."

"You're very kind, my dear—what is your name?" said the frog magician.

"Mildred Hubble," replied Mildred. "What's yours?"

"Algernon—er—something-or-other Webb. Isn't that awful?" said the frog magician. "Do you know I can't remember the first bit, I've been here so long? What was it now? Bowen-Webb? Stone-Webb? Or was it Webbley-Stone? I'm sorry, child, I've completely forgotten. Oh, dear, it was all so very long ago. I must say, sometimes I'd give *anything* to have a proper old-fashioned tea again, one gets so fed up with flies and water boatmen. Every now and then I can see it all so clearly; a nice log fire and a little round table with a tablecloth, and hot toast with great slabs of butter, and crumpets with honey all oozing out of the little holes, and a china cup with steaming tea—"

The memory was too much for him and he erupted into loud, desperate sobs, a pitiful sound to hear.

Mildred hopped next to him and patted him with a half-visible arm. "Don't cry, Mr. Algernon, sir," she said comfortingly. "You *shall* have crumpets for tea again; don't you worry. It'll be all right; I promise it will."

# CHAPTER SEVEN

IGHT had fallen and the pupils of the academy were all in bed. That is to say, most of the pupils were in bed. Enid had sneaked into Maud's room for a quick conference about Mildred. It was bitterly cold in the cell-like bedroom, and the two girls were huddled on the bed, wrapped in blankets, with cats draped over their feet to keep

out the cold. (Maud was taking care of Mildred's tabby.)

"Well, I give up," said Enid. "If she has run away, she's left every single piece of clothing behind, even her cardigan, so she must be frozen solid by now."

"She hasn't run away," said Maud. "She wouldn't have gone just because H.B. told her off. Anyway, she's not likely to have run away without old Tabby here, especially as that was why H.B. was cross in the first place. It just doesn't make sense. No, I'm quite sure that Ethel knows something about it. Don't you remember what she said to Mildred? No one insults my family and gets away with it. Well I think she's done something really awful to Mildred."

"Like what?" asked Enid.

Just at that moment, the cats all leapt to their feet with their fur on end and looked in the direction of the door. The girls exchanged nervous glances, thinking that it

must be Miss Hardbroom come to repri-
mand them for being out of bed. Maud
crept to the door and opened it very slowly.

Outside in the shadowy corridor was
the little frog which had escaped from the
potion laboratory. Maud and Enid could
tell it was the same one because its feet had
not yet reappeared.

Mildred hopped inside and was picked
up by Maud, who took her over to Enid.

Tabby immediately began nuzzling up
against the frog in a very friendly way,

unlike the other two cats who kept in the background, backs arched and humming frantically.

"How strange, Enid!" said Maud. "Look at Tabby. It seems as if they've met before."

The two witches suddenly looked at each other in horror.

"Oh, *no*!" they exclaimed at the same time.

"It can't be!" gasped Maud. "Or can it?"

"I think it might be," replied Enid grimly. She took the frog from Maud and held it up near her face.

"Are you—" she began, but before she could finish, the little frog was leaping up and down, nodding its head and croaking so loudly that the girls were afraid someone would hear.

"Sssh!" whispered Enid. "Calm down, for goodness' sake. Now then, are you our very good friend, Mildred Hubble?"

There was no doubt about it, from the nodding and mad capering, that here was the answer to Mildred's sudden disappearance.

"Did Ethel do it?" asked Maud.

More nodding and croaking was the answer.

*"Right!"* said Maud. "Come on, Enid."

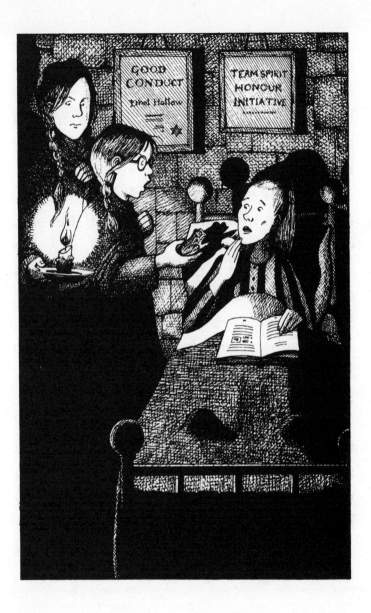

Ethel was not asleep, either. She was sitting up in bed learning the chant which was to be tested the next day. She nearly leapt through the ceiling when the door opened and Maud and Enid marched menacingly into the room.

"Recognize this?" asked Maud, holding out the frog. "Remind you of anyone, does it?"

Ethel turned white as a sheet. "I—I don't know *what* you're talking about," she said.

"All right," said Maud, "then we're off to Miss Hardbroom. Come on, Enid. Sorry to have bothered you, Ethel."

"No!" cried Ethel. "It's Mildred, isn't it? Oh, thank goodness you found her. I didn't mean her to run off and get lost. I just wanted to give her a fright, that's all. Come here and let me take off the spell."

"Hold on a moment," said Enid. "I think we'd *better* get Miss Hardbroom. I mean, how are we going to explain where Mildred's been?"

"Let's tell her in the morning," wheedled Ethel. "She'll be in a dreadful mood if we disturb her tonight. Anyway, I'm sure poor Mildred here can't wait a moment longer."

Ethel spoke the words of the spell, and at once Mildred was standing before them.

"Thanks for nothing, Ethel Hallow," she said, rubbing her arms and legs. "Gosh, it feels really odd to be this big again. Oh Maud, it was so awful in the potion lab, I really thought I'd had it."

The door opened like a thunderclap, and there stood Miss Hardbroom.

"Having a little party, are we, girls?" she inquired drily. "Ah, Mildred, I see you've decided to rejoin us at last. We hope you have had a pleasant time wherever you have been. Would it be too much, perhaps, to inquire exactly where you have been, hmm?"

The three friends looked desperately at Ethel, who stepped forward with a smirk flickering at the corners of her mouth.

"I caught Mildred creeping down the corridor with Maud and Enid here," she said innocently. "So I invited them into my room and I was just coming to fetch you, Miss Hardbroom."

*"Ethel!"* exclaimed Maud, Enid and Mildred together.

"That's not *true*, Miss Hardbroom," squeaked Mildred indignantly. "Ethel turned me into a frog, and that's where I've been for the last day, and it was her fault. She's only just changed me back."

"I did *not*," lied Ethel, sounding convincingly angry. "I wouldn't do such a thing, unlike some people around here," she added under her breath, referring to the time when Mildred had accidentally changed Ethel into a pig during their first term at the school.

"Mildred," said Miss Hardbroom, "you will write out five hundred times, in perfect handwriting, 'I must learn to curb my imagination and to —' good gracious, girl! What on earth has happened to your feet?"

They all looked and saw that Mildred's feet, still recovering from the invisibility potion, had not yet reappeared, even though she had changed back to her usual self.

"That *proves* it!" exclaimed Mildred joyfully. "Miss Hardbroom, I was the frog in the potion laboratory, the one you found in the corridor, and the potion I took is only just wearing off—that's why I haven't any feet at the moment. Oh, yes! And to prove it even more, I can tell you that you have a handkerchief, a whistle, and a notebook with a rubber band round it in your pocket!"

Miss Hardbroom turned to Ethel.

*"Well?"* she asked, in tones so terrifying that all four of her pupils shrank back against the wall.

"I—I, well—I—she *had* insulted my f-family, Miss Hardb-broom," said Ethel feebly. "And I really didn't mean her to

run off like that. I only meant to give her a scare. I didn't mean . . ." she trailed into silence.

"Ethel, Mildred," said Miss Hardbroom, "you will both come to my room first thing in the morning before breakfast. Now get along to bed at once, all of you."

Their form mistress ushered the three friends to their separate rooms. Mildred's room was the last of all.

"Let us hope that your feet are in the correct place by the morning, Mildred," said Miss Hardbroom frostily, as Mildred hastened inside and closed the door.

# CHAPTER EIGHT

SHORTLY after the rising-bell had been rung, Ethel and Mildred were waiting anxiously outside Miss Hardbroom's door. It was the first time that Ethel had been summoned to her form mistress for any reason other than praise.

"It's *your* fault, Mildred Hubble," she muttered, as they paced up and down the corridor. "If you hadn't told that stupid story to Sybil and upset her, I wouldn't have done it to you. Anyway, I really *was* going to take the spell off straightaway, but of course *you* had to go hopping off and get caught and land us in this mess."

"*You've* got a nerve, Ethel Hallow!" said Mildred. "You just can't ever admit you might be wrong, can you? It wasn't exactly fun being pursued round the potion lab and shoved into jars. It wouldn't occur to you that—"

The door opened and Miss Hardbroom beckoned them inside.

"Sit," she barked, indicating two chairs opposite her desk. They all sat down.

"It *wasn't* my fault, Miss Hardbroom!" Ethel blurted out. "Mildred Hubble told my little sister this story about first-years being changed into frogs by the teachers. She even told Sybil that the frog in the school *pond* was enchanted, and poor Sybil was in such a state that I thought someone ought to teach Mildred a lesson."

"It wasn't exactly like that, Miss Hardbroom," said Mildred. "I'd gone up to Ethel's sister to cheer her up because she was looking so miserable. I didn't know—"

"I have heard quite enough excuses," interrupted Miss Hardbroom, "and I do not wish to hear any more. Frankly, I am not in the least bit interested in whose fault the incident was.

"The reason I have called you both here is to remind you that you are now second-year witches, and I do not expect this ridiculous feud between you two girls to continue. Do you understand?"

"Yes, Miss Hardbroom," replied Ethel and Mildred meekly.

"Ethel," continued Miss Hardbroom, "just because you happen to be an excellent scholar and one of the most helpful members of my class, I do not expect you to lie your way out of a situation when it has become awkward. Do you understand this?"

"Yes, Miss Hardbroom," said Ethel.

"Neither," said Miss Hardbroom, "do I expect you to contravene the Witches' Code, rule number seven, paragraph two, by changing your fellows into any sort of animal for whatever reason. Do you understand *that*?"

"Yes, Miss Hardbroom," said Ethel.

"Good," said Miss Hardbroom. "Then you will understand why I am giving you one hundred lines which will say, 'I must tell the truth at all times.' "

She turned her attention to Mildred. "Mildred, I would ask you to refrain from tormenting the first-years with untrue horror stories about the academy, and to make some attempt to *think*—if that is possible—before you embark upon any more madcap escapades."

"Yes, Miss Hardbroom," replied Mildred. "Oh, and Miss Hardbroom, I've just remembered, there *is* a frog in the pond and it really *is* someone under enchantment. I *know* it sounds like another made-up story—"

"Mildred Hubble," said Miss Hardbroom wearily, "what have I just said to you? No, don't attempt to answer. I expect you've completely forgotten already, haven't you? Sometimes I feel that any attempt to communicate with you is an utter waste of time.

"Now I have said all that I wish to say to you girls except, Mildred, that you will write one hundred lines which will say, 'I must try very hard not to be quite so silly.' Now hurry along to breakfast, girls. That will be all."

Mildred was now faced with the impossible task of convincing someone that there was an elderly magician in the pond. She tried to tell Maud and Enid, but they had had enough of frog stories, particularly as Mildred had actually admitted to them, at the time, that the story she had told Sybil was not true.

It seemed quite hopeless. The only way of getting to a magician was at the celebrations on Hallowe'en night, but after the broomstick display, which Mildred had ruined the year before, she felt very worried about creating any more havoc in that direction.

Mildred spent a lot of time by the pond telling the frog magician that she hadn't forgotten him and that she would get him out if it was the last thing she did. He always kept a distance from her, but she felt sure he knew who she was. Looking at his froggy face, half-submerged in the murky water, it was hard to believe that he really was anything more than an ordinary frog, and Mildred could see why no one had recognized her when she was in the same plight.

# CHAPTER NINE

 WEEK before the Hallowe'en celebration, Miss Hardbroom entered the classroom, looking grim.

"Sit, girls," she said, looking round severely at the rows of pupils. "I have here a letter from the chief magician, Mr. Hellibore, who presides over the Hallowe'en festivities each year. In this letter he specifically requests that the girls responsible for the utter fiasco which *should* have been our broomstick display last year are to be kept away from this year's display so that he can relax and enjoy the events taking place. Those two girls were Ethel Hallow and Mildred Hubble. It is true that the incident was not actually Mildred's fault, for once, because Ethel *had* cast a spell on the broomstick which Mildred was using, but in view of our little *chat* this morning, girls"—here she darted a glance at Ethel and Mildred, who wriggled uncomfortably in their seats—"I feel this is a most fitting punishment for both of you. As you retire to your beds at dusk on the eve of Hallowe'en, perhaps you might ponder upon the exciting evening you *could* have been enjoying and resolve to end this ridiculous feud at last."

Mildred was very upset at her exclusion from Hallowe'en for several reasons. One was the awful unfairness of it all, as it really hadn't been her fault that Ethel had cast a bad spell on the broomstick she had lent to Mildred, thus ruining the display.

Also it would be very hard to stay in bed and miss the evening's fun. But, worst of all, she would not be able to take her unfortunate friend to be changed back to his normal self, and this was the only night of the whole year when she would be in the presence of a magician.

There was only one thing to do. She would have to persuade someone to change places with her, and if that didn't work, she would have to kidnap someone and *force* them to swap places. Even the thought of this plan seemed dreadful to Mildred, who could see how such a course of action was fraught with danger, but there really was no alternative if she was to help the frog magician.

Maud and Enid were the obvious people to ask, but they flatly refused.

"You must be barmy, Mildred," exclaimed Maud. "H.B. would *slaughter* us if we got caught. Anyway, what's it *for*? I mean if *I* was you, I'd just put up with it and stay in bed. Enid and I will describe it all when we come back."

"Look, Maud," pleaded Mildred, "I *know* it's hard for you to believe me, but that frog in the pond really *is* a magician, and he can only be changed back by another magician. If you don't want to change places with me, then couldn't you take him yourself and ask the chief magician for help? *Please.*"

"No way!" said Maud and Enid together.

"Honestly, Mil," said Enid gently, "I know it must have been awful when you were turned into a frog, what with the narrow squeak in the potion lab and everything, but don't you think perhaps you're getting a little *obsessed* with frogs and ponds? Maud and I have seen you down there chatting away to the empty water. Perhaps a nice evening in bed might be good for you, after all."

Mildred stomped away feeling desperate. If Maud and Enid thought she was mad and wouldn't help her, then no one would, and the only course of action was to go ahead with the kidnapping plan. Mildred quailed at the prospect.

The morning of the celebrations dawned, and the whole day was given over to ironing best robes, practising on broomsticks, and chanting. Mildred and Ethel sat miserably at their desks, feeling very left out of all the bustle.

As the afternoon drew to a close, Mildred crept downstairs and out into the darkening yard. She hurried to the pond and peered among the reeds to see if her friend was visible.

"Mr. Algernon, sir," she whispered, "come out, Mr. Algernon. I've got something to tell you, sir."

For a moment the water lay dark and still, then a ripple touched the surface and two green eyes appeared like periscopes.

"Oh, Mr. Algernon!" exclaimed Mildred with relief, and before he had time to hide away under a stone, as he usually did, she shot a hand into the water and scooped

him up. He did not want to be caught at
all, and although Mildred told him where
they were going and tried to soothe him,
he struggled madly and looked at her with
great suspicion. Mildred slid him carefully
into her pocket and raced up the stairs to
her room, where she transferred him to a
small box with holes in the lid, which she
had prepared specially for the journey.

"You'll be all right there for a while,"
she told him, tying on the lid with a piece
of string. "You mustn't worry. It'll be all
right—I promise."

The next step was to find and kidnap a suitable victim. Of course, the easiest thing to do would have been to change someone into a frog or snail or some other small creature which could easily be kept hidden in a box until she returned. But, to be honest, Mildred felt that there had been quite enough animal enchantments in the school to last a lifetime, and it seemed a less desperate measure to do a nice, straightforward kidnap, where at least you could see exactly what was happening.

As she came out of her room, Mildred saw a third-year witch named Griselda Blackwood approaching down the corridor, carrying her cat.

"Excuse me!" gasped Mildred. "Er—I was wondering if you could just come and help me for a moment?"

"Whatever for?" asked Griselda. "What's the matter, Mildred? You look quite pale."

"There's something horrible under my

bed!" exclaimed Mildred. "Could you come and help me get it out?"

"Something horrible?" repeated Griselda, drawing back in alarm. "Why, what do you mean *something horrible*? You can't really expect me to go fishing about underneath your bed if I don't even know what I might find under it, now can you?"

"It's a—er—beetle!" replied Mildred triumphantly. "I've got this *thing* about beetles. A horrid brown one with pincers ran up my pyjama leg once and I've never got over it. Please help me, Griselda. I won't get a wink of sleep otherwise."

"A beetle!" laughed Griselda. "Is that all? I thought it must be a tarantula at least with all the fuss you're making. Come on, then."

While Griselda was half under the bed, feeling about, Mildred very stealthily tied her bootlaces together.

"I can't seem to find anything," said Griselda, shuffling out and sitting back on her heels.

As quick as a flash, Mildred pulled out a lasso of rope which she had hidden in a drawer and slipped it over the astonished girl's head and shoulders, yanking it tightly enough to bind her arms to her sides. Before the poor victim had a chance to scream, Mildred had tied a gag around her mouth. As a last resort, Griselda tried to run for it, but of course her bootlaces were tied together, so she fell flat on her back.

"I'm really ever so sorry to do this to you," apologized Mildred humbly, as she tied Griselda's ankles together with her sash. "It's really in a very good cause and I'll explain everything to you later when I get back. I'm so sorry, I really am. I don't usually go around doing this sort of thing. I hope you don't mind *too* dreadfully."

Griselda stared up at Mildred from the floor with horror.

"Mmmmmmmmm!" she raged through the gag. "Mm-mmm, mmmm-mm, mm, mm, mm, mm, mmmm!"

Mildred pulled some bedclothes from her bed and covered Griselda tenderly.

"There really isn't any point in shouting," said Mildred, putting a pillow underneath the victim's head. "No one can hear you. They're all getting ready in the playground. I'll borrow your cat if you don't mind. Mine's awful on a broom, and anyway it's too easy to recognize."

Mildred changed from her ordinary school uniform to the best robes, which the girls always wore for special occasions. She unplaited her hair and shook it out loose. (The whole school, including the teachers, always wore their hair loose when they dressed in their best robes.) She put on her cape and turned up the collar and pulled her hat low over her eyes.

There was a soft "meeow" from the top of the wardrobe, and Mildred saw her little tabby cat watching reproachfully as she prepared to go without it.

"Oh, Tabby," said Mildred, reaching up and tickling its chin, "I can't take you or the whole school will recognize us."

She picked up the box with the frog magician in it and wedged it into her cape pocket. Then she slung Griselda's cat around her shoulders and took her broomstick from its place against the wall.

"Good-bye, Griselda," said Mildred, slinking out of the room feeling like a criminal. "I won't be long, and then I'll explain everything and you won't be cross anymore."

# CHAPTER TEN

UT OF the window, as she hastened down the spiral staircase, Mildred saw the fires which were being lit in the ruins of the old castle where the celebrations were always held. Her heart pounded as she joined the throng of girls in the gloomy yard, all looking most dramatic with their hair loose and their long black robes and witches' hats.

"Thank goodness, it's almost dark," thought Mildred, tagging on to the end of form three as their form mistress counted them all.

"Is everyone accounted for?" asked Miss Cackle.

All the form mistresses answered "yes" in turn, and the pupils began their flight to the castle.

The school receded into the distance as the pupils skimmed above the treetops, and Mildred was grateful that no talking was allowed in flight, so nobody could ask her any awkward questions. The borrowed cat was a wonderful balancer, and Mildred felt rather disloyal as she found herself thinking how nice it would be to have a well-behaved sleek black cat which she could feel proud of.

Back at the academy, Ethel sat fuming in bed and watched from her window as the pupils rose like a flock of bats into the twilight and sailed away without her. She picked up her candle and decided to

go along to Mildred's room and have a grumble at her.

Outside Mildred's room, Ethel pressed her ear against the door and was surprised to hear a strange noise from within.

"Mildred?" called Ethel, knocking softly. The noise grew louder.

"Mmmmmm! Mmmm, mm, mmm!" Ethel opened the door and held up her candle to reveal the awful sight of Mildred's victim trussed up on the floor.

"What on earth has happened to you?" gasped Ethel, untying the gag and pulling at the knots in the sash and rope.

"It's that Mildred Hubble!" said Griselda, who was almost in tears. "She must have gone berserk. She got me in here under false pretences, tied me up, stole my cat, and went to the display in my place. Honestly, Ethel, she sounded really mad, wittering on about beetles up her pyjama leg and suchlike. Whatever shall we do?"

"Go after her, of course!" answered Ethel, delighted at the thought of the praise they would get when they revealed Mildred's wicked behaviour.

"Come on, Griselda, I'll change into my outdoor clothes and meet you in the yard with my broom in five minutes. We'll have to hurry. Goodness knows what that girl is planning!"

"All right," agreed Griselda. "I'll run and fetch my broom."

Meanwhile, the academy was alighting on the castle hillside and being welcomed by the chief magician and all the other witches and magicians. The chief magician,

Mr. Hellibore, looked most imposing in his purple robe embroidered with moons and stars and a tall, pointed hat. Mildred would have been absolutely thrilled by it all if she had not been so terrified of the task ahead of her.

There was a long delay between the pupils' arrival and the commencement of the displays and chanting, during which Miss Cackle and the teachers greeted friends and acquaintances, and the girls all stood to attention, being neat and well behaved and a credit to the school.

Suddenly there was a commotion in the sky, and everyone looked up to see Ethel and Griselda swooping down on their brooms, waving and shouting.

"Mildred Hubble's down there!" shrieked Ethel.

"She kidnapped me!" yelled Griselda. "And she tied me up, so she could come in my place!"

"That's enough now, girls, thank you," ordered Miss Cackle, who was not at all pleased at such unseemly shrieking from her girls.

Miss Hardbroom strode across to the rows of pupils, and Mildred pulled her hat even lower over her face. From under the brim she could see the chief magician nearby, looking rather puzzled at all the shouting.

"If you *are* here, Mildred," said Miss Hardbroom, "I would advise you to step forward at *once* and explain yourself."

The pupils all began looking round at each other, and Mildred knew there was little time before someone recognized her. There was no alternative but to make a dash to the magician before anyone could catch her. Summoning every scrap of courage, Mildred suddenly barged through the rows of pupils and threw herself in front of Mr. Hellibore.

"Please forgive me, Your Honour," she said, thrusting the box containing her friend into his hands. "I know you didn't want me to come here tonight, but there is an enchanted magician in that box and I promised him that I would get him to you so that you could change him back. I'm so sorry to cause such a lot of trouble, but I didn't know what else to do."

"What on earth is all this nonsense about?" asked the chief magician sternly. "And are my eyes deceiving me or are you not the girl who *ruined* the broomstick display last year? If so—"

"We do apologize most humbly, Your Honour," grovelled Miss Hardbroom, seizing Mildred's arm in a vice-like grip. "The girl seems to have taken leave of her senses—"

"I *haven't*, Miss Hardbroom!" interrupted Mildred. "*Please*, Your Honour, Mr. Hellibore, sir, it really *is* a magician. His name is Algernon Webb-something, Stonely-Webb, oh *something* like that, only he couldn't quite remember. He's been a frog for simply ages."

"Good gracious me!" exclaimed Mr. Hellibore. "Do you know, Miss Hardbroom, it might just be Algernon Rowan-Webb. He was my roommate in the days when your school was used as a sort of summer camp for magicians, and he actually *did* disappear one day and we all thought he must have gone home. But it was *decades* ago — why, the poor chap! If you'll excuse me, Miss Hardbroom."

Mildred kept her eyes firmly closed as the chief magician opened the box and intoned the release spell. Suddenly there was a gasp from the crowd. Mildred opened her eyes and breathed a huge sigh of relief.

Standing in front of them was an extremely old man with a beard that trailed on the ground and long flowing white hair. He was very bent over and was rubbing his eyes as if he couldn't quite believe it.

"*Algy*, old chap!" exclaimed the chief

magician with joy. "It's *Egbert,* your old friend. Don't you remember?"

"Egbert!" replied Algernon. "Yes, of course I remember, though you were a lot younger in those days. Excuse me a moment; I shall have to sit down. It's all a bit much for me after all these years as a frog. My legs and arms feel awfully cramped. Egbert Hellibore! Well, well, what a piece of luck."

"The luck came from your little friend here," said Mr. Hellibore, placing a hand on Mildred's shoulder. "This child braved all our displeasure to bring you here."

Mildred felt very shy as the vast crowd fell silent and every pair of eyes swivelled in her direction.

"Do you remember me, Mr. Rowan-Webb, sir?" asked Mildred. "We were frogs together."

"*Remember* you?" repeated Algernon. "My dear Mildred, how could I ever forget you? No one ever had a truer friend. Without your help I would have been a frog forever. And please call me Algernon."

"Well, Miss Hardbroom," said Mr. Hellibore, "we can hardly send the girl back to school again after this act of heroism, now can we?"

Miss Hardbroom ground her teeth and managed a horribly false smile. "Whatever you wish, Your Honour," she replied.

"Is there anything you would like as a reward, my child?" asked Mr. Hellibore, smiling kindly down at Mildred.

Mildred thought for a moment. "Oh, yes, sir!" she replied. "There *is* one thing."

She stepped forward on tiptoe and whispered in his ear.

"Is that *all*?" said Mr. Hellibore with a laugh. He leaned across and quietly told the ancient magician what Mildred had asked for. Algernon smiled dreamily. "What a wonderful memory you have, my dear," he said. "Yes, that would be very nice, very nice indeed."

The crowd watched in fascinated silence as Mr. Hellibore snapped his fingers and a small table appeared in his hand, set with a white tablecloth, tea for three, and a huge plate of toast, crumpets, and butter. Algernon peered at the table, then snapped *his* fingers and a pot of honey appeared. "Mustn't forget *that*," he commented as he set it on the table. And, with a glow of pride, Mildred walked away arm-in-arm with the two most important people at the celebrations, to have a proper old-fashioned tea by the nearest bonfire.